today's promises

today's promises

S. R. GREY

ISBN-10: 0986156590

ISBN-13: 978-0-9861565-9-5

Editing: Hot Tree Editing

Cover Design: ©Hang Le

Formatting:

E.M. TIPPETTS
BOOK DESIGNS

emtippettsbookdesigns.com

Author's Note

Thank you for taking this journey with me. Flynn and Jaynie's story is fictional, but, in reality, there are far too many real stories of abuse within the foster care system. Thank you to those individuals I spoke with, who shared their own experiences so readily. This story is for you…and for all the children who have no voice.

Chapter One

Flynn

"No, no, no, no…"

Jaynie thrashes and kicks at my legs, which until a few seconds ago were snugly entwined with hers under the soft homemade quilt on our bed. "Jaynie, wake up!" I cry out.

I jump back just in time to avoid a sharp kick to the shins.

Sighing, I reach over to shake her shoulder, to rouse her from whatever horrific nightmare plagues her tonight.

But before my hand touches her, she wakes on her own.

Glancing over at me, her expression, clear even in the shadows of our small rented room, turns from panic to relief. "Flynn," she breathes out. "God, I thought I was alone again. I'm so glad you're here."

"Of course I'm here, sweetheart. Don't worry. I'm not going anywhere, never again."

Jaynie starts to cry, her tears soon soaking through the front of her tank top and my T-shirt. "I was so scared, Flynn," she croaks out.

"I know, sweetheart. I know."

I hold on to her more tightly. It's all I can do. But it's good...and it's more than enough. There's no need for strung-together words or lengthy explanations. I know all too well the substance of Jaynie's bad dreams.

Hell, I have the same nightmares myself—terrible, all-too-real snippets from our time in foster care, brought back to life in living color, deep in the land of bad dreams.

I did six years' worth of time in foster care, and Jaynie, she was in for four. If it sounds like I'm talking prison sentences, instead of the foster care system, it's because living under the state's too-oft indifferent care, enduring a life of being shuffled from one crappy home to the next... Well, it kind of is like doing time.

Only thing is you haven't committed any crime.

But you sure as hell feel like you did.

Jaynie lifts my arm. Sliding out from under me, she rises from our bed.

"Where're you going?" I ask.

Turning back to me, she mutters flatly, "Bathroom."

When I start to protest, she gives me a small smile. It's meant to reassure me that all is cool, even though I know it's not. "I'll be back in a minute, okay?"

What can I do? "Yeah, okay," I mumble.

I watch as Jaynie pads barefoot the short distance from our bed to the tiny bathroom connected to our room. Her auburn hair sways in time with her slim hips, hips covered by navy-blue boy shorts that were pushed aside earlier so we could engage in a hasty, but intense, coupling.

It's like that sometimes with us, desperate and raw, remnants from our past.

When the bathroom door closes, I hear Jaynie turning the inside latch. She thinks she can lock her secrets in with her, keep them hidden from me.

But she can't.

I know what she does in there. After she empties her bladder, Jaynie will slide down to the cold linoleum floor and binge-eat several candy bars she keeps ferreted away. See, I found her secret stash the other morning, the day after I arrived in Lawrence. I should tell you at this point that I was a few months late in getting here. I *should* have arrived back in the fall, along with Jaynie. This small West Virginia town was always meant to be our destination…if we ever had to run.

And we had to. Run, that is.

I was delayed by our former foster 'mom,' a middle-aged woman named Mrs. Lowry, who now sits alongside her equally rotten daughter, Allison, in prison. Mrs. Lowry was blackmailing me, and I ended up stuck in Forsaken, the dying town we used to live in a few miles away, for four extra months.

But I'm here with Jaynie now, for good.

So, back to the morning following my arrival…

After spending the night in Jaynie's bed—which I guess is now my bed as well, seeing as we live together—I found myself looking for a disposable razor so I could shave. That's when I came upon a few dozen candy bars. They were stuffed way in the back of the cabinet under the sink, behind several rolls of toilet paper and a few bottles of cleaners. I counted at least forty-seven Hershey's…and numerous empty wrappers.

As I sifted through the tattered, chocolate-smudged debris, my intention being to deposit all the trash in the little pail by our toilet, I got to thinking about the nightmare Jaynie had had that morning, just before dawn.

After I'd rocked her till she was no longer sobbing, she'd excused herself to go to the bathroom, where she spent an exorbitantly long time.

It only took me a minute to put two and two together.

I didn't mention anything to her that morning. And I still haven't.

Shit, I understand. Hoarding food doesn't sound so weird once you've experienced true starvation. And starve we did at our last foster care home, especially during the final two months.

Remembering the hard times, I promptly helped myself to a candy bar that morning, despite the fact Jaynie had, minutes before, yelled into the bathroom that our landlord, Bill Delmont, who also happens to be our employer, had breakfast waiting for us downstairs in his sandwich shop.

But enough of all that.

I'm brought back to the present when I hear Jaynie drop something in the bathroom. Scrubbing a hand down my face, I'm torn over how best to help her. It's hard to help someone, I've found, when your own life is a freaking mess.

I hear Jaynie tearing open a candy bar, and I mutter, "Fuck."

Rolling to my back, I rest my arm over my eyes. I've eaten plenty lately, but my stomach, as if on cue, begins to rumble. It's like all this thinking about starving has reminded me of what it actually feels like to go days without food.

We are still both *so* fucked-up. Will we ever heal?

"Fuck it." I throw back the quilt and head toward the bathroom. "Jaynie…" I rap on the door, once, twice, three times. "Let me in. Please."

The door opens slowly, revealing my broken girl. She stands before me, a half-eaten candy bar in one hand and chocolate smudged all over her chin.

"Busted," I say. I'm trying to tease her to lighten the mood, but it sounds lame and pathetic.

"Sorry," she mumbles.

I reach out and, using my thumb, wipe away evidence of her binge. "Don't be silly. There's no need for apologies. I was only kidding around."

"All right, Flynn."

When my stomach growls again, there's no hiding I'm in the same boat as her. We're like Pavlov's freaking dogs, I swear.

"Hey," I say softly, "think you could spare one for me?"

Smiling for the first time since I caught her red-handed—or chocolate-chinned, as it were—her deep green eyes sparkle.

Pulling me into the bathroom, she says, "Just get in here, Flynn."

We spend the next ten minutes gorging on chocolate. And the reason is simple—when you've lived the lives we've lived, all within eighteen short years, you don't take chances.

You cover your bases. You live prepared. You eat when you can since you never know when the food might run out, or when it will be withheld from you.

The bottom line is that you absolutely *must* be ready for things to turn bad, because they always fucking do.

"Hey, can I have another?" I ask as I polish off candy bar number three.

Jaynie hands me five more and then wisely suggests I look for a spot to hide four of them.

"You know," she says, shrugging, "in case my stash ever runs out."

"I'll find a good place," I promise her. "And then I'll let you know where it is."

"You do that, Flynn," she replies, her eyes holding mine. "But after you tell me, don't let anyone else know where you hid them. Like…ever."

I nod, agreeing to her terms. Hell, it makes perfect sense.

What can I say—old habits die hard.

Chapter Two

Jaynie

Bill Delmont, who saved my ass the night I showed up at his door sopping-wet last October, has turned out to be a godsend.

Bill understands the downtrodden since he's led a rough life of his own. He was once homeless, but the tide eventually turned for him. He now calls himself a successful businessman. And he is, too; he owns the sandwich shop in Lawrence where Flynn and I work.

He's a really good man, the kind of guy who makes it his ongoing mission to give back. That's why he was quick to give me a job at the Delmont Deli, only an hour after I arrived.

He helped Flynn when he got here, too. In fact, it was the very next morning, during a big, delicious breakfast Bill had prepared, that he offered Flynn a job manning the counters and cleaning up around here.

Flynn accepted. He and I divvy up shifts, usually working on alternating days. We were hoping to work together to make double the wages, but a sandwich shop this small, located in a tiny West

Virginia town, is not nearly busy enough to justify two employees behind the counter at any one time.

It happens sometimes, but not on any regular basis.

That's why this afternoon, while I'm working my shift, wiping tables in the front of the shop, Flynn is at the counter in the back, perusing the local want ads in the newspaper.

Bill offered Flynn use of his computer to conduct a search for higher-wage and more-hours employment, but he declined. He believes he'll have better luck with the local paper.

When I asked Flynn why he thought the paper would be a better option than checking online, he told me, "Not too many guys searching for the type of work I'm looking into have access to a computer. Some companies post jobs online, sure, but a lot of the local places know that to get a ton of applicants, they better damn well invest in a good old-fashioned want ad."

"Makes sense," I replied, nodding.

After I finish wiping down the last of the tables, up by the big picture window facing the street, I head to the back of the shop.

Plopping down on a plushy chair behind where Flynn is still perusing ads, I ask, "Any luck?"

Spinning his stool to face me, he rubs his hands down his face. "Eh, I don't know. There aren't as many listings as I'd hoped."

"No good leads, then?" I ask, deflated.

"Actually," Flynn says, perking up, "I did see an ad for a pretty decent construction job. It's Monday through Friday, nine to five. Good wages too, babe."

"Well, that sounds promising," I cross one jean-clad leg over the other. "Where is this promising new job?"

Flynn lowers his gaze, like he knows I'm not going to like the answer. "Uh, it's over in Forsaken," he says.

I make a face. I *don't* like that answer.

Forsaken isn't far, but it happens to be the town we ran away from. And frankly, I have no intentions of ever going back. I don't want Flynn hanging out over there either, whether it's for work or whatever reason. He was stuck in that blasted town the entire time Mrs. Lowry was blackmailing him.

"That place holds too many bad memories," I mutter.

"Jaynie..." Flynn peers over at me, growing frustration clear on his face. "We could still live here in Lawrence. You'd never have to step one foot in Forsaken if you didn't want to."

"And I don't," I scoff, shaking my head.

"Okay, so what's the problem?"

"Well, for one, how do you intend to get to work all the way over there every single day? It's not like we own a car."

"And we're not *ever* going to own a car, Jaynie. Not if I can't land a job paying more than working the counter in this place."

I sigh, accepting the truth. "You do have a point," I reluctantly admit.

Even though I hate, hate, *hate* the idea of Flynn working over in that wretched town five days a week, his argument for taking the job is valid. We've discussed it numerous times, and the fact remains that unless we plan on living in the single room above the sandwich shop forever, and unless we intend on relying on public transportation indefinitely, we need more cash coming in.

Flynn's previously somber expression turns hopeful now that he sees I'm slowly coming around, albeit begrudgingly so.

"So here's what I'm thinking..." he begins.

I can almost see the wheels turning in his head as he works out a plan. It's endearing, one of the many qualities I missed about him the past four months.

"Until we've saved enough for a car," Flynn goes on, "I'll just take the bus. There's one that heads over to Forsaken every morning and returns every evening. It couldn't get any easier, Jaynie. Almost like it's meant to be."

S. R. GREY

Oh, he's laying it on thick. And I'm not surprised.

Flynn won't do this unless I support him. It's the way we work. And for all the wheels and cogs to run smoothly in this relationship, we also don't hold each other back. Despite my own misgivings, which are really my own damn issues, I buck up and make myself muster some enthusiasm for Flynn's plan.

It's the least I can do after everything he's sacrificed for me.

"Yeah," I say, my smile forced but present. "Once we have a car, even if it's some old jalopy, you can use that to get to work. I'd imagine that'd save us a lot on bus fares in the long run, right?"

"There is that," Flynn says, shooting me a winning smile.

I smile back.

Damn, I am so easy, always won over by Flynn's charm. And how could I not be? The guy may have been dealt a bad hand in some aspects of life—like losing his brother at his dad's hands and ending up in foster care—but he sure is blessed in the looks department.

He wows me every day with his beauty, inside and out.

"So," he goes on, oblivious to my inner fawning, "you're absolutely sure that you're fully onboard with me applying for this job?"

"Yes." I stand and go to him.

Wedging my body between his strong thighs, clad in faded jeans, I reach out and touch his shirt. It's the same steel-gray color as his eyes.

As I give him a good once-over, I notice something. "Hey, you're wearing the same clothes you had on when I first met you." I narrow my eyes, but all in good fun. "Did you plan that to win me over if I bailed on this Forsaken job thing?"

"No, no way." He shakes his head, the ends of his sandy-brown hair brushing the back of his tee.

"Your hair is darker," I say, touching his face. "And this scruff on your jaw grows in thicker than it used to."

"Faster, too," he adds.

9

"Yeah," I murmur.

I don't mention all the other changes, some due simply to better nutrition. Flynn's gotten much taller, and he's stronger than the day I met him—*much* stronger. Working construction while he was stuck in Forsaken has given him broad shoulders and far more muscle mass.

I'm changed as well. I'm still thinner than I should be, but I do have boobs and an ass, finally.

Not starving sure does make a difference in a person's appearance.

"Oh, the lives we've led," I whisper.

"And to think we're only eighteen," Flynn replies.

Sighing, I admit, "Some days I feel so much older, Flynn."

"Yeah, babe. Me, too."

Placing my hands on his shoulders and feeling all the hard muscles flex beneath, I tell this man, "I love you so much, Flynn O'Neill."

"I love you even more, Jaynie Cumberland."

I touch my nose to his. "Mmm, I don't know if that's possible."

With his hands trailing down to cup the curve of my ass, he murmurs, "When's your shift done?"

Wrought with innuendo, I know Flynn wants me.

As for me… Well, I pretty much want Flynn all the time. And now is no exception.

"I have one more hour to go," I say, brushing my lips suggestively over his.

He releases me and slips from the stool. Brow raised, he starts backing away. "Meet me up in our bed the second you're done?"

"Yes, okay."

"Good. Let me *show* you just how much I love you, Jaynie-girl."

I let out a little groan. "Gah, Flynn. You can't do that to me. Not now. Not when I have a whole other hour left."

"It'll go fast," he says, winking as he spins around and heads for the stairs leading up to our apartment.

"It better," I call out.

I spend the next hour counting down the minutes till four o'clock.

At 4:01 on the nose, I race up the stairs.

Five minutes later, Flynn starts to show me just how much he loves me.

And... Damn, I have no words.

He shows me again at 4:35, and then again at 5:04.

Oh, and once more at...

Oh hell, I think you get the picture.

Chapter Three

Flynn

There are no nightmares for Jaynie—or me—on Friday night. It's not because I found a cure or anything, although I sure as hell wish there was one and I *could* find it. But no such luck. The lack of bad dreams in this case is simply the result of not sleeping.

I'm awake most of the night, tossing and turning. And that, in turn, keeps Jaynie awake.

"Sorry, babe," I mutter as I turn to her sometime after five in the morning.

She touches my cheek. "It's fine, Flynn. But you have no reason to be nervous. You know this, right?"

"Yeah… I guess."

Despite Jaynie's reassuring words—and I know they're true—I just can't relax. I am nervous as hell because tomorrow I'll be visiting with a little boy and a little girl who couldn't be any more my siblings than if we shared blood. Cody and Callie are the twins who lived with Jaynie and me in our last foster home. And I'm finally going to see them again.

"Jesus, I love those kids," I say.

"I know, Flynn." Jaynie rubs my shoulder, trying to comfort me.
Still, I'm anxious. "I haven't seen the twins in six months."

"It doesn't matter," she insists. "They love you so much, Flynn.
And love like that doesn't fade, not even with time."

I hope she's right. Six months of not seeing the twins is longer
than my time away from Jaynie. Allison Lowry, Mrs. Lowry's bitch
of a daughter, ripped Cody and Callie away from us when she sent
them to a group home back in August. Luckily, another of our foster
siblings, an awesome girl named Mandy, rescued the kids and is
currently fostering them up in Morgantown.

I've missed the twins a lot since I last laid eyes on them, and
I think of them every fucking day. Hell, I hope they remember me
when we reunite, especially Cody. He's always reminded me of the
little brother I once loved so very much.

"When will the twins be nine?" I ask Jaynie as I try to focus on
something other than my little brother, Galen. "I should know that,"
I add, "but I suck at birthdays and shit."

I flip over to my back and stretch out diagonally across our bed.
Jaynie sits up so I can lay my head in her lap. She starts combing her
fingers through my hair. She's still trying to help me relax, though the
movement is probably soothing to her, as well.

"Their birthday's not till April," she replies softly.

"That's right." I glance up at her. "I remember now. Last year
Mandy and I saved a couple of those crappy nutrition bars, the ones
Mrs. Lowry used to give us for breakfast—"

"Ugh," Jaynie interjects.

I nod, agreeing completely. "I know. Gross, right? But that was
all we had. Anyway, Mandy found a pack of old birthday candles up
in that old barn in the fields and we loaded up each bar with four
candles apiece, making it eight in all. Then we sang 'Happy Birthday'

to the twins."

"Aw, that's sweet. I bet Cody and Callie loved that."

"Yeah, I think they were happy we remembered their day. Wish we could've done more for them, though, you know?"

Jaynie knows I'm plagued with regrets, and her hand stills. "Hey," she says. "You and Mandy did what you could, Flynn. You have to stop beating yourself up when it comes to things in the past. Not to mention, all is not lost. We can make their birthday special *this* year. Let's drive up to Mandy's that day, okay? We can all do something fun together. We should have a car by then."

She pauses, letting it sink in for me that her car comment is her supporting me in going for that job in Forsaken, despite how much she despises that town.

I look up at her. "Hey, thanks, babe. For everything, I mean. I really don't know how I made it through all those horrible months without you around, keeping me sane."

"I was always there with you," she whispers.

And in a way, she was.

I choke up a little at those memories of the bad days in the past. But Jaynie comforts me with words of reassurance that we'll never again be apart.

Eventually, we maneuver till we're lying on our sides, face-to-face. With one of her legs draped over mine, I marvel at how things have changed from when we first met.

"Hard to believe there was once a time I couldn't touch you," I say.

My hand is on her hip and I squeeze lightly.

"I know," she replies, a little breathless. "But I sure do love how you touch me now."

Jaynie pushes her body against mine suggestively, and, chuckling, I nod down to our pressed-together selves. "We've come a long way, haven't we?"

"We have," she agrees, smiling. And then, in a contemplative tone, and with her body going lax, she says, "There is one thing, though... Something I think about a lot."

"What is it?" I ask.

"I don't think I could *ever* be this way with anyone but you, Flynn. Really, I don't."

My male-possessiveness side rejoices, but then my heart twists when she lets out a sob and adds, "That's one reason why you can never leave me again, okay?"

When Jaynie cries harder, I pull her close to me. "Hey, hey, it's all right. I told you before that I'm not going anywhere. Not now, or ever. In fact, now that I'm here, you're never going to get rid of me."

"Good," she chokes out against my shoulder.

God, I don't think my reassuring will ever be enough. It takes a lot of words to lessen the pain caused from one's actions.

Caressing Jaynie's back through the thin tank top she's wearing, I try to lighten the dismal pallor that's fallen over us like a dark veil.

"Oh, you say that you want me around *now*," I begin. "But I bet you a million dollars there'll come a day when you're so sick of me that you'll be asking me to go find myself a man-cave, or some other place you can send me to when I'm getting on your last nerve."

"Never, never, never," she insists.

Jaynie proceeds to grasp and hold on to the back of my tee like I'm her life raft. And I guess, in a way, I am.

"That will never happen," she hisses adamantly.

"Aw, Jaynie, I was just kidding around," I assure her.

"I know, Flynn. But I swear to you I will never get sick of having you around. I exist for you."

"And I for you," I reply as I bury my nose in her auburn hair and breathe in this girl that I love.

I may be her life raft, but she sure is mine as well.

15

Chapter Four

Jaynie

Flynn can't keep his hands still on the steering wheel. Tapping along to the low music playing in the background, flexing his fingers, stretching out his hands—I swear it's something every few minutes.

And we still have half an hour to go till we reach our destination.

"Hmm, someone sure is getting in their hand exercises today," I tease.

I'm trying to add some levity to ease Flynn's anxiety, but my attempt at humor goes over like a lead balloon.

"Okay," I murmur.

Flynn chews at his lip, then glances over at me. "I'm good," he says, with false bravado. "I feel totally confident about this visit with the twins."

"Sure, Flynn," I reply.

His gaze remains fixed my way, and I have to point to a stretch of windy interstate up ahead and remind him he's driving.

"Uh, eyes on the road, mister. Bill was nice enough to loan us

16

his car for the day. We should probably try to return it to him in one piece."

"Ha-ha, Jaynie," Flynn remarks. But he does re-focus to the road, even if it is with more finger-tapping on the wheel.

Placing my hand on his leg, the denim of his jeans worn to a buttery smoothness that's comforting in its own way, I say softly, "Hey, quit worrying so much. Remember what I told you last night. The twins are going to be *thrilled* to see you."

Sighing, he replies, "I just hope you're right. It's been so long. And you know how kids forget things."

"Not these kids, Flynn," I murmur.

When he lets out a ragged sigh, I squeeze his leg. Hopefully I'm reassuring him that things are going to be just fine.

Flynn can't see what I see. He's blinded by too much guilt—unnecessarily so, of course—for not being able to see the twins for so long.

It doesn't matter.

I know for a fact the twins can't wait to see Flynn, especially Cody. When I was up in Morgantown recently, visiting with them and Mandy, not only did both kids remember Flynn—which, really, how could they ever forget him?—but Cody actually thought he might be with me that day.

When he realized I'd come alone, he was so disappointed.

It broke my heart.

When I think on it more intently, that entire day was bittersweet. Back then I didn't know if *any* of us would ever again see Flynn. All I knew at that time was that he was making a conscious decision to stay away. It was only after he and I reunited that I found out the truth—that the evil Mrs. Lowry was keeping Flynn from all of us.

I should've known that was the case. I bear my own guilt for trusting him so little. Fucking bitch Mrs. Lowry and her machinations.

"I'm so glad she's in prison," I spit out, my venom fueled by the memory of my days away from Flynn and time that can never be recaptured.

We don't speak much of the horrors we suffered at the Lowry house, but Flynn knows exactly whom I'm referring to.

"Don't worry," he replies, his jaw suddenly set firm. "That bitch will live out the rest of her days in a prison cell. Allison will be locked up for a long time too."

Yeah, but for how long? I think as a wave of nausea hits me.

Allison was the reason we had to run on the night that turned out to be our final hours spent in foster care. And what rough hours they were. After Allison kicked the living shit out of me, I lost the baby I was carrying. That tiny snuffed-out life was my child, and Flynn's.

One thing for certain—I will *never* forgive that bitch for taking away what was ours.

Overwhelmed, I twist so I can stare out the window and not think of anything. "I just need a minute," I tell Flynn.

He says nothing. He just gives me my space. Good, he knows I need this quiet time. But my quiet time is short-lived when memories creep back to the forefront of my mind.

A light rain begins to fall and droplets, not unlike tears, bead on the glass.

I peer past the raindrops—tears—to the scenery passing by. Even those small glimpses, like images on hyperdrive, it's still too much. Every damn thing we pass is a reminder of my past—like the way the cliffs on the side of the interstate look so similar to the precipice I plunged from that final, horrible night.

Memories of ice-cold water and the raging current wash over me, and I shudder in response.

One of my recurring nightmares is that I don't make it out of the water. Instead of finding a way of working with the current, as I did, I am held under by unseen hands—Allison's hands.

I know it's her pushing me down because, as my lungs fill with icy water, all I hear is her laughing… and laughing… and laughing.

I blink, panicked that my view has turned watery.

But no, wait.

My eyes are filled with tears, not with the water from the river that exists so vividly in my head.

Way off in the background, like an echo, I hear Flynn, desperately pleading, "Jaynie… Jaynie…. Talk to me, babe. You're shaking. Are you all right?"

I'm not all right, not at all. But I'm a little better when he pulls over to the side of the highway. There, it's the whir of the cars flying by that returns me to reality.

Flynn unbuckles his seat belt, leans over, and wraps me in his arms. "Hey, hey," he whispers in my hair.

Better, better. Flynn always makes me feel better.

"I'm sorry I mentioned her name, okay?"

"It's not your fault," I mutter. "I just… I just feel like I'm always living in fear. I can't stop thinking that Allison will come and find me someday. So she can finish the job."

"She's in prison, Jaynie," he reminds me.

"Yeah, but really, when you think about it, how much longer is she going to stay locked up?"

Flynn has no answer, and I sob harder against him.

My fear is not unfounded; that's what is so frightening. Mrs. Lowry, Allison's mother, is serving a long sentence, with little possibility for parole. She will most likely remain behind bars for her entire life, as she committed far more crimes than Allison, crimes with stiffer sentences. Mrs. Lowry did things like embezzle hundreds of thousands of dollars from innocent people. Allison, on the other hand, was found guilty of one crime only—fraud. She used to cash the state checks meant for her mom to use for our care.

What a joke.

Sadly—and because sometimes the world works in grossly unfair ways—neither Lowry woman was ever charged with any kind of crime related to the torment of the kids they fostered.

In the end, it came down to their word against ours.

It kills me, though, to think Allison's fraud is classified as a non-violent felony. It is, but, still… How ironic, considering what all she did to me. Nonetheless, here we are, all these months later, facing the cold hard truth that Allison won't remain in prison forever. Far from it, in fact. With prison overcrowding plaguing the local correctional facilities, Flynn and I *know* Allison has a high likelihood of being up for parole as early as sometime next year.

And that is far too soon for me.

Flynn is trying so hard to comfort me as I pour out all these thoughts. Still, I can't stop a fresh new round of tears from starting up.

"Whatever happens, we'll get through it," he tells me, while he strokes my back and holds me gently. Kind of like I'm a fragile doll and may break at any time.

"I can be strong in so many ways," I say, as if to reassure not only him, but myself.

"I know, babe."

"It's just…" I lean back and wipe my nose as I try to pull it together. "The hatred Allison has for me is so real and so heavy sometimes that when I let it truly sink in, like how I'm doing now, it just pulls at me. It ends up weighing me down, Flynn, and that cuts into my strength."

"I know, Jaynie," he says. "I completely understand."

Thank God someone does.

I peer into his steady eyes—gray, like the sky today. "Hey, I'm sorry I lost it."

"Don't apologize, babe. We've talked about this thing with Allison maybe getting out a hundred times. Just know that when…and if…it happens, we'll manage."

I sigh. "I know. But seriously, Flynn, what the hell are we going to do if she really is released early?"

Settling back on his side, he signals to merge back onto the highway. "Let's just hope her parole is denied. Every...fucking... time."

"And if it's not?" I throw out.

Releasing a heavy breath, he says, "I don't know what we'll do then, Jaynie. I just don't know."

I can't respond, because sometimes there are just no adequate words.

Chapter Five

Flynn

I drop to my knees on the floor of Mandy's modest but tidy living room, and Cody—*my* Cody—flies into my arms.

In that moment, everything is right in the world. Jaynie was right; this kid loves me. I had nothing to worry about.

I sigh, content as I hold on to a little boy who means the world to me.

And that is when I have a revelation: *This* is my life.

It will never be perfect, and I'll never be able to completely erase the pain. But I have this—these little snippets of joy I can grab on to…and hold close to my heart. These are the moments that will get me through the pretty much daily grind of bullshit life always seems to dole out.

"Flynnie, Flynnie." Cody's arms tighten around me, and this is so fucking right. "I love you *sooo* much," I am informed.

I'm holding on to that heartwarming snippet.

"I love you, too, bud," I reply, a little misty-eyed.

"I missed you," Cody says. "Lots and lots and lots."

I'm snatching up that one as well.

I then tell the kid, "I missed you too, little man. More than you could ever imagine."

Cody loosens his arms from around my neck and leans back just enough to show me his displeased expression.

"Uh-oh," I say. "What's that look all about?"

"Why you no come visit me sooner?" His tone is at once accusatory and disappointed.

Shit, time to think fast. "I would have visited you, Cody, but I was sort of tied up."

"With work stuff?" he asks.

His big brown eyes are so innocent, so accepting of any explanation I'm about to offer, anything whatsoever. Kids, they kill me with their resilience to bounce back. If only Jaynie and I could've stayed innocent long enough to have been rescued, before all the bad stuff.

Softly, I murmur, "Yeah, it was something like that."

I can't say much more. I'm sure as hell not about to share with Cody that our wicked foster mother kept me away from him, and everyone else. That would scare him to death. I'm hoping Mrs. Lowry and her hellhole of a home are becoming nothing but distant memories for him...and for his sister, Callie, too.

Speaking of Callie, she's hanging back, standing behind Cody, giving him time to reconnect. Jaynie and Mandy have retired to the kitchen, to give me time alone with the twins, I'm sure.

Holding out my hand, I say to Callie, "Hey, I missed you too, you know."

"You did?" she hesitantly asks.

"Yes." I nod emphatically. "Like every single day, Miss Callie."

Smiling brightly, she takes my hand. And ten seconds later she's laughing, nestling in next to her brother, all of us hugging. "I missed you so much, Flynn," she says.

My heart is touched. And, just like that, I have another snippet of joy to stow away.

"Aw, sweetheart," I whisper. "I missed you and your brother like you wouldn't believe. I'm back to stay though now. And that means we can see each other a lot more often from here on out."

"Are you *really* back for good?" Callie sounds unsure and takes a step back, exiting from our hug. Cody, however, stays glued to me.

"Yes," I reply, with what I hope is a tone of certainty she will hear and believe. "I'm back for good. I promise."

A few more minutes pass, and then Jaynie and Mandy rejoin us in the living room.

"You okay?" Jaynie asks when she sees me swiping at my eyes.

Mandy is off to the side, chatting with the kids about what they'd like for lunch.

Amid excited requests for grilled cheese and tomato soup, I tell Jaynie, "Yeah, I'm great. It all went way better than I expected."

"I tried to tell you not to be so consumed with worry, you silly man."

I laugh. "Yeah, yeah, you did. And you were right, babe."

"Always," she says, bumping my hip.

"Lesson learned. I should always trust Jaynie."

"You bet your ass."

The next several hours fly by, and the next thing I know our entire day has been spent with Mandy and the twins. It's a little like old times, but way better.

For one thing, there's plenty of food.

Mandy cooks up a huge fried chicken dinner that everyone digs into. Accompaniments that are quickly devoured include creamy mashed potatoes, peas, and biscuits with lots of butter.

"I love butter," Cody exclaims at the dinner table. He then proceeds to lick all the butter off his biscuit.

"Gross," Callie says as she makes a sour face.

But not two seconds later, it's her who is slathering extra butter on her own biscuit and handing it over to Cody.

She says to him, "Here, I dare you to eat this one. It has even more butter than yours did."

Mandy, Jaynie, and I share a bittersweet smile, as we know what's really going on. Callie daring her brother to eat another buttery biscuit may sound like a typical kid dare, but really it's so much more.

Cody isn't starving anymore, but Callie remembers all too clearly when he was.

Cody eats the biscuit, plus three more—mine, Jaynie's, and Mandy's.

Yeah, we all remember.

After dinner, Mandy and Jaynie start clearing dishes. I offer to help, but both girls insist I spend more time catching up with the twins.

That's fine with me, as I soon discover I have a lot of catching up to do.

Cody unwittingly reminds me of this fact when he says to me, "Hey, Flynnie. Did you know we go to school now? Like, to a *real* school, with compooters and everything."

"No way, little dude," I exclaim, trying to sound shocked.

"Yes, way," he reiterates, nodding.

"Do you like your real school?" I ask.

"Uh-huh."

Callie rolls her eyes. "Of course he likes his school, Flynn. He gets to stay in a special class all day, where they draw and play on computers and have fun. *I'm* in real third grade, where we do *real* school stuff."

I close my eyes, and my heart feels like it's being squeezed in my chest.

See, Jaynie, Mandy, and I homeschooled the twins as best as we could while we were in foster care. Still, I don't think it was ever really enough. Callie was fine, excelling in all the subjects we taught. Cody, however... Well, he was a different story. He just needed much more help than what we were able to give him.

Shit.

It pisses me off that we just didn't have the resources. But now I'm so fucking happy to hear he's in a class that suits his learning style. Though I'd be lying if I didn't admit it still kills me that we couldn't provide more for him.

There was just so much we weren't equipped to handle.

Nonetheless, I can't let old regrets bring me down. Not today.

And they won't.

Despite a few bittersweet moments, our reunion runs smoothly. The only glitch is that Mandy's boyfriend, Josh, ends up stuck at the plant he works at.

That kind of sucks, seeing as Josh is now the twins' foster dad. To say I was hoping to meet him would be an understatement.

"He'll be home after eleven," Mandy informs me, a few hours after dinner, when I again bring up the subject. "You're welcome to hang around till then."

All five of us are chilling in the living room, our stomachs full from Mandy's tasty meal.

Though I'd love nothing more than to meet who we were always told was the love of Mandy's life—a guy who, by the way the twins' eyes light up when his name is mentioned, treats the children extremely well—Jaynie and I have to decline the offer.

"I'd love to stick around," I reply. "But we promised Bill we'd have his ride back no later than ten."

Jaynie, seated next to me on the couch, adds, "Speaking of which, it's already after eight. We should probably hit the road soon to give ourselves plenty of time to get back."

The twins, who are lying on the floor, playing a board game, jump up when they hear we're leaving.

"No leave yet, Flynnie," Cody begs as he comes over and plops down on my lap.

"I have to, bud."

Wide eyes fill with hope as he asks, "You come back tomorrow, then?"

This is where it blows that we don't yet have our own car.

"I'm afraid we can't, little man," I try to explain. "We borrowed the car we drove up in."

"So borrow it again," Callie interjects.

She's crawled into Jaynie's lap, and is peering over at me like *what's the problem with that?*

As Jaynie curls the ends of Callie's long charcoal-black hair around her finger, she tells her, "Once we have our own car, honey, we can visit more often. And we can stay as long as we like."

"I guess I can wait for whenever that happens," this precocious child concedes.

With a dim pallor of disappointment cast over the final minutes of our visit, we begin the long process of saying our good-byes.

Jaynie and I hug the twins for a solid ten minutes, and then Mandy walks us to the door. The twins stay behind in the living room to, upon Mandy's suggestion, resume their board game.

"Hey, guys, hold up a sec." Mandy grabs a jacket from a hook near the door and adds, "Let me walk out with you to your car."

It's kind of clear by now that she wants to tell us something out of earshot of the kids. Jaynie looks over at me, like I may have an idea as to what Mandy wants to talk about.

I have no clue, so I shrug and shake my head.

Once we're out in the tiny, postage-stamp front yard, I turn to Mandy and ask, "So, what's up?"

She glances back at the house. I guess to make sure the twins haven't followed us out.

When she's sure the coast is clear, she says, her voice still hushed, "I just want to give you guys a heads-up. You should hear this from me first, not someone else."

"What's going on?" Jaynie asks, her brow creasing with concern.

Mandy makes a face. "Uh, well, here's the thing… Josh recently heard from an old friend who's now a state trooper that the authorities are re-opening an investigation into what kind of environment Mrs. Lowry was providing for us foster kids the past several years."

"A horrible one," I scoff.

Jaynie's face pales. "We aren't going to have to testify or anything, right?"

That's Jaynie's big fear.

Every terrible thing we endured is still so fresh and raw for all of us, but especially for Jaynie. She suffered the worst at the hands of our captors, and that's really what they were. We were all trapped up there at the Lowry house. I could talk if I needed to, about all the shit we went through, but I know for a fact Jaynie isn't anywhere near that point yet.

Testifying isn't a worry, though, at least not for today.

We realize this when Mandy explains: "There's a detective on the case, but he's not looking into what happened during *our* time at the Lowry house. Not that it wasn't awful, what we went through, but it seems"—she lowers her voice another notch—"something much worse may have occurred before any of us ever lived there."

"Shit, Mandy." I take a step back. "Like what?"

"Yeah, what could be worse than what we went through?" Jaynie chimes in.

Mandy wraps her arms around herself, like she's now chilled by more than the cool night air. I understand. I'm feeling kind of icy myself.

"A girl went missing," Mandy says. "A girl Mrs. Lowry was fostering about seven years ago."

"So back when she first started fostering, then," I remark.

"Yeah, back then." Mandy nods. "I guess state records had this girl listed as having been placed elsewhere, following the days she spent at the Lowry house. Apparently, though, that was some kind of mix-up."

I muse, "I guess they're going through everything now with a fine-toothed comb."

"Yeah, only because Allison and Mrs. Lowry were convicted of felonies," Jaynie interjects, shaking her head. "You know, those crimes that involved money people lost. Not anything to do with how kids, like us, were physically hurt and mistreated. I swear," she practically spits out. "It's always about the goddamn money, isn't it?"

"Maybe not this time," Mandy says, sending a sad, small smile Jaynie's way. "The girl who used to live at the Lowrys, the one involved in the mix-up, they're really looking into this pretty intensely. Apparently, her name was similar to someone else's in the system. And *that* girl is the one the state was keeping track of."

"That's one hell of a mix-up," I snort, disgusted at the total ineptitude of the state system.

"I know, right?" Mandy shakes her head. "Anyway, the authorities think this girl may have never left the Lowrys."

I watch Jaynie as she swallows hard.

"How old was she?" I ask, my voice cracking at the implications of what Mandy is telling us.

Bowing her head, she says, "Sixteen."

"Maybe she ran away?" I offer, grasping at any explanation so Jaynie doesn't have to hear this. Her nightmares are horrid enough.

But Mandy, her eyes moving from me to Jaynie, then back to me, crushes that hope when she says, "Mmm, I don't think so, Flynn. The last place this unaccounted-for girl was ever seen was at Mrs. Lowry's house."

"What are you saying?" Jaynie says, at last.

Her voice is more strained than I've ever heard it before. So I reach for her hand, to offer any comfort I can.

Jaynie is trembling when her hand slips into mine.

And frankly, I start to shake as well, especially when Mandy says, "Someone up on that property, either Mrs. Lowry or Allison, had to have killed that poor girl. And then they probably hid the body."

Chapter Six

Jaynie

"Shit, Flynn, this is bad. Really bad."

Those are the first words out of my mouth when we settle into Bill's car.

Flynn buckles his seat belt and closes his eyes. I'm sure he's imagining some poor girl, a girl like me, meeting her untimely end at the hands of Mrs. Lowry, or that bitch, Allison.

Shuddering, he says, "God, I hope it's not true."

I let out a scoff of disbelief. "Oh, I'm sure it's true. Think about it. Think how close we came to being finished off up there." I make a sound of disgust. "We're not talking about kind benefactors here."

"True." Flynn scrubs his hand down his face. "I'm sure something bad did happen to that girl."

Thinking of how Allison treated us so much worse than her mother did, I say, "I bet Allison did it. She's vicious and violent."

I know firsthand the extent of Allison's rage.

Flynn agrees with me, but then, when he sees how worked up

I'm becoming, he says, "Let's talk about something else on the ride home."

"Yeah, that works for me."

On the drive back to Lawrence, I try with all my heart to push all thoughts of Allison and her evildoings to the back of my mind. And I do pretty well, until that night when a nightmare wakes me up.

After dreaming of Allison kicking me in the abdomen, and thusly killing the child who was growing within me, Flynn rocks me back to sleep with words of comfort. His own tears intermingle with mine, and we press our cheeks together and cry for what could have been.

"It's over, though, Jaynie," he tells me. "She can never hurt you that bad ever again."

But it seems she can when—a couple of days following my nightmare—I show up for an appointment at the local free clinic. The plan is to finally start on birth control. But it may be a moot point when the repercussions of the violence Allison inflicted on me rears its ugly head.

I've been thinking all this time that Flynn and I have just been lucky. I mean, we have sex all the time, right? And I've not yet become pregnant.

And now I know why.

I am informed, during the routine exam, that I have severe scarring in my uterus, scarring that was never there before, scarring that may render me infertile for the rest of my life.

I am numb.

I'm still given a contraception shot on the slim chance the doctor could be wrong.

But I know she's not.

I leave the clinic in a daze, devastated by the possibility that not only has Allison taken away my baby, but now, thanks to her brutality, I may *never* call myself a mother.

I'm scheduled to work that evening in the sandwich shop, but as soon as I get back I request the night off. Flynn had that stupid interview in Forsaken today, and when I wander upstairs I'm sick to find he's still not home.

"Oh, great," I mutter to myself in the lonely silence of our bedroom. "I can see how relying on the bus to get to and from work is going to make for some long-ass days for everyone."

Flynn finally arrives home when it's well after seven.

By that time, I am miserable.

With the news of today so fresh, and Mandy's update the other night still in my head, I can't think of anything other than the horrible things that have happened over at the Lowry's place.

Flynn finds me curled up in our bed, with my face wet from all the crying jags that keep coming in waves. I tell him everything, and he holds me close as I sob into his flannel shirt. When I'm finally spent, I collapse against his firm chest, my reserves depleted.

But while my own tears have ebbed, Flynn's have just begun.

Twisting to peer up at him, just as he tries to disguise a sob as a cough, I say, "You should find someone else. You deserve to be with a girl who can give you children someday."

He hastily wipes away teary evidence of his sorrow, but his gray eyes remain sad, even as he declares, "Jaynie, don't be ridiculous. It's you I love, not what you can or can't give me. And if it ends up just me and you for the rest of our lives, I accept that. In fact, I'd count a long life with you as a gift."

I shake my head, all set to start anew at convincing him of my sound reasoning. But Flynn silences me with an index finger to my lips. "Hey, no more talk of me finding another girl. I love you...and only you. It will *always* be you, Jaynie-bird."

Will it be, though? What if Flynn changes his mind in five years? Well, if that happens, so be it. Until that day comes, I will stand by him.

In a strangled tone racked with sorrow, I whisper, "I love you so much, Flynn. I'm just—I'm just…so damn sorry."

"Aw, Jaynie…"

We hold each other close for a long, long time.

Eventually, though, we move on to talk of his interview. It's not that our sorrow has passed. It's just that we have no choice but to accept our fate and move forward.

Clearing my throat, I say to Flynn, "Hey, you never told me what happened at your interview this afternoon. Did you get the job?"

"Yeah," he replies. "I sure did. They seemed really happy to have me."

"Of course they'd be happy. You're a good, reliable employee." I take a breath, blow it out. "So… When do you start?"

"Tomorrow," he replies.

I sit up. "What kind of construction project will you be working on?" I ask, truly curious.

Still resting his head on the pillow we were sharing, Flynn peers up at me. "I'll be working on the first phase of some new apartment complex," he says.

Forsaken is a rundown dump, so to say I'm surprised is an understatement.

"A new apartment complex is being built in that town?" I scoff. "You've got to be kidding me."

"Nope, it's all true," he says. "But they're being built over on the outskirts of town. Never fear, Jaynie-dear. Forsaken remains the shithole it's always been."

"No surprise there," I murmur, rolling my eyes.

Flynn sits up next to me. When he leans over me to reach for a pack of gum over on the nightstand—a pack I just now notice— my eyes widen. That gum definitely wasn't there earlier. He must've bought it today, before or after his interview.

That worries me. Flynn only chews gum when he's staving off a craving for a cigarette. See, he started smoking again when he was stuck in Forsaken. But since we've reunited, he hasn't smoked once.

Suspicious of what else went on today in that freaking town, I carefully ask, "What's with the gum?"

Leaning back and peeling the foil from a stick of chalky green, he says, "I bought the gum this afternoon." His eyes meet mine, and he comes clean. "It was either chew gum or smoke a cigarette, Jaynie."

"Wait." I twist to face him. "I thought you said the interview was a breeze."

"It was. It's just that being back there… Well, you know how it is. Being in the thick of things, close to all the shit that happened, it just kind of stirs it all up inside you, you know?"

"I do know," I say, since I do. "But that's what I meant when I originally told you I was against this job over there. One damn afternoon in that crappy town and you're already stressed to the max."

Around the piece of gum he's chomping on—spearmint, by the smell of it—Flynn says the same thing he's maintained from the start. "We need the money, Jaynie."

"I don't know if it's worth this grief," I counter. "Maybe you should turn down this particular job. You can look for work in other places. You already know how much I absolutely hate the idea of you spending any time at all over in that evil town."

"It's not the town that hurt us," he replies. "Plus, I won't be working in Forsaken, not technically. It's just that the interview was there." He draws a breath, and then releases it slowly, like he's calming himself. "Like I told you already, the job itself is on the outskirts of town. It's almost completely outside the city limits."

"I know you said all that, but…"

"What?"

"Bad things seem to happen all around that place. It's like there should be some kind of a sign." I make air quotes. "'Stay away', it should read. And also, 'oh, by the way, give yourself a one-mile radius, just to be sure.'"

I'm kidding, of course. Well, sort of.

Flynn, determined to make our lives better at all costs, insists, "This is a good job, Jaynie. It's a full-time, steady gig. One with better-than-decent pay."

When he can't look me in the eye, though, I suspect something more is at play here.

That prompts me to ask, "Are you sure nothing else happened over there today?"

"Oh, yeah, there was one thing," Flynn says, as nonchalant as ever. "I did run in to an old buddy. It happened when I came out of the job center."

Aha!

There's only one old friend Flynn could possibly have run in to, so it's with confidence that I say, "Crick, right?"

"Yep." He nods. "He drove right by me, and I waved him down. We ended up talking, and then grabbing a quick lunch."

I've yet to meet Crick, but that doesn't mean I don't want to. He was a good friend to Flynn during the months he was stuck in Forsaken.

Seeing Crick wouldn't upset Flynn, though—not like this—so I press, "Did you guys go anywhere else? Besides to lunch, that is?"

Flynn schools his features to an expression that reveals nothing, making it hard for me to discern whether he's telling the truth. Especially when he says, "No. We just ate lunch together. Then we went our separate ways."

Hmm... "You plan to keep in touch?"

"Yeah, I'm sure we will." Flynn shrugs. "We exchanged digits, plus I'm bound to see him around."

"Ugh." I topple to my side and plant my face in a pillow.

"What now?"

"The same thing as before," I say, sighing. "I still just can't believe you're going to be spending so much time in and around that freaking town."

I peek up, and find Flynn scrubbing a hand down his face.

"Jaynie, please, stop," he whispers. "What choice do we have? I mean, really?" He gestures around our small place. At the bare wooden floor, the tiny closet in the corner, the small, outdated attached bath. "Do you want to live in this little room forever? Do you want to take the bus for the next five years?"

"No," I mutter.

"Okay then. Case closed."

Accepting that this is our only real option, I say, "You have to promise me one thing, then. Can you at least do that?"

Reaching down and tucking a wayward lock of hair behind my ear, he says, "Anything, babe."

"Promise me you'll stay far, far away from the Lowry property."

Flynn has to look away when he says, "Okay, yeah, sure."

Crap. I know then and there that something bad definitely happened in Forsaken this afternoon. However, I can't keep questioning him. Not now, not after all the emotional upheaval of this goddamn day.

What I need is a break…and maybe a candy bar.

"Hey," I say as I scoot to the edge of the bed. "I think I'm going to take a quick shower before we go to sleep."

Flynn seems completely distracted when he replies, "Yeah, okay, Jaynie."

He doesn't try to stop me, even though he has to see the guilt on my face. Still, he just lets me go to the bathroom, where he knows I'm about to pig out.

I know for a fact, then and there, that the promise he just made, the one to stay away from the Lowry property, is destined, if it hasn't already, to become what so many of our promises end up to be— simply another one of tomorrow's lies.

Chapter Seven

Flynn

I can't bring myself to share with Jaynie *everything* that happened during the time I spent over in Forsaken today. I want to tell her, I do. But I can't, not just yet.

See, that promise I just made to stay off the Lowry property? Well, it's already been broken. In fact, it's the events that occurred this afternoon that have me craving a smoke, to the point now that I may lose my goddamn mind.

Reaching for another stick of gum, to prevent what I fear is about to become inevitable, I check the bathroom door to make sure it's still closed.

It is.

No surprise there.

Jaynie went in a couple minutes ago to take a shower before bed. Or that's what she claimed she was doing. Though water is running in the bathtub, I suspect it's all a cover. She's probably sitting on the floor, chowing down on multiple candy bars.

We all have our demons.

"Yeah, like you and cigarettes," I remind myself.

When I start taking off my jeans, readying for bed myself. I come upon the small card, a business card, in the back pocket.

Shit, I have to hide this from Jaynie, or she'll flip.

It's bound to come out eventually, though. Yeah, soon enough I'll have to confess where I went after lunch with Crick.

Most of what I told Jaynie was how it really went down. Just not *all* of it.

The interview went well, as I expressed, but it took far less time than I expected. Afterward I had a lot of time to kill, before the evening bus was due to take me back to Lawrence. I considered walking home, for about a minute, but then I ran across Crick.

My old friend kept me sane during my time away from Jaynie. And despite his past—he was once addicted to meth—he's a stand-up dude. I was happy to see him again, as the only sad part when I left Forsaken to return to Jaynie, was me thinking I'd never again see my good friend.

But there he was this afternoon, driving down the main drag in a cable company truck. I was standing in front of the job center, a spot where we used to hang out and drink coffee and smoke cigarettes before work.

I started waving like a madman, hailing him down. "Hey, Crick!" I called out. "Whoa, man, hold up."

He slammed on the brakes when he saw me. And then he pulled over to the curb, to just beyond where I was standing.

Smiling, I ran up the sidewalk and skidded to a stop by his truck.

Reaching over the front bench seat, he rolled down the passenger-side window.

"Flynn, my man," he said, breaking into a genuinely happy smile. "You look glad to see me."

"I am, man. I am."

"So, I gotta ask," he went on. "What the hell are you doing back in this goddamn dirtbag town?"

"Looking for work," I replied, chuckling.

"Really, huh?"

"Yep."

He nodded to the job center, his stringy, dishwater-blond hair moving right along with his bobbing head. "They have anything for you in there?"

"Actually, they did. I saw an ad in the paper the other day, and it said, 'come to the job center, interview on the spot.'"

"Great. How'd it go?"

Smiling, I informed Crick. "I got hired on the spot. You're looking at one of the newest workers on the construction crew that'll be putting up those fancy apartments out on Route Nine-Ten. You know the ones, right? There've been signs everywhere, bragging about how nice they'll be."

"Yeah, I know the ones you mean," he said. "So, when you start?"

"Tomorrow." I rapped my fist on the roof of his truck. "But enough about me. What's this new ride all about? You work for the cable company now?"

Crick looked proud as ever when he said, "I do, kid. Right as snow, I do."

I chuckled. Damn, I'd missed this guy. Crick's a trip, always spouting off his own crazy-ass mixed-up versions of well-known sayings.

Instead of correcting him and saying *I think the saying goes 'right as rain,'* I said, "That's great, man."

Crick then mentioned how it was his lunch hour.

Since I had plenty of time to spare, I said, "Well, I got nothing to do right now."

He then asked if I wanted to join him, and I said, "Hell, yes."

When I hopped in the truck, he warned, "Now, it ain't gonna be nothing fancy. I only got 'nough money for one of them cheap fast food value meal deals."

"Hey, I hear 'ya. Cheap works for me." Sighing, I added, "I'm kind of low on funds myself."

We ended up rolling through the drive-thru of the local McDonald's. Crick ordered two of those value meal deals, and he asked for them to be super-sized. To this day, it cracks me up that he stays skinny as fuck when he eats like a horse. I had to give him some good-natured grief about it, of course.

After I finished my burger, I said, "Dude, you are a machine. Where do you put it all?"

"Fast metabolism," he replied, polishing off his extra-large fries.

"Hell, you must've been skin and bones when you were on meth," I remarked.

"Fuck, kid, I looked like one of them there skeletons you hang on the door at Halloween."

"Shit."

Crick lowered his voice. "I remember you looking like a bag of bones at one time too. And it wasn't all that long ago."

"Yeah, I know." I blew out a breath. "Only thing different was my days as a bag of bones wasn't from drug use. Allison Lowry was literally starving me and Jaynie before we got out of that place."

Crick knows all about our past, and he shook his head, disgusted. "Yeah, I remember you telling me about that crazy bitch and the things she was doin' to y'all. That was some fucked-up shit right there." He gestured to my jeans and flannel shirt, to the clothes that no longer hang on my body but instead showcase how bulked up I've become. "Look at you now, though, kid," he said. "You're big and strong and healthy. And those are the things that matter. You beat that bitch, yeah?"

"Yeah, it's amazing what good nutrition can do," I deadpanned.

Crick, fumbling with his smokes, nodded.

Lighting up, he held the pack out to me. "You want one?" he asked from around the filter of the cigarette he'd wedged between his lips.

"No." I shook my head. "I'm good."

And I *was* good, at that time.

It was the events that followed that freaked me the fuck out.

Chapter Eight

Jaynie

When I emerge from the bathroom, fresh from the shower I eventually got around to taking, my hair is wet, and my skin is damp and sticking to my oversized sleep tee.

Since he didn't check on me, not once, I know for certain something is up with Flynn. He's still so damn distracted, in fact, that he doesn't even notice that I'm back in the room.

Seated on the edge of the bed, in just his boxer briefs, he's peering down intently at a small piece of cardstock in his hand.

A business card, maybe?

"What's that?" I ask.

"Oh, hey, you're back." Flynn quickly opens the drawer of the nightstand next to our bed and tosses the card in. "And that"—he gestures to the drawer—"was nothing."

I let out a little snort. "Since when do we save 'nothing'?" He shrugs, and I add, "That's not a very good hiding spot if you plan on keeping whatever that is a secret from me."

He falls backward onto the bed and covers his face with his arm. "Jaynie," he says on a sigh, "can you just let this one go?"

"Not a chance, bud." I walk over to the bed.

As I stretch out next to him, lying on my stomach, I remind him, "We don't keep secrets from one another, remember?"

He groans, then sneaks a peek over at me from under his arm. I touch the little crescent-shaped scar beneath his right eye, a present from his biological father, when he got too enthusiastic with his belt.

"If something's going on, Flynn, you should want to talk to me about it."

"Fuck." He jumps up from the bed and heads over to the closet where he hung his coat when he first came in. After a few seconds of frantically fishing through the pockets, he pulls out a slightly crumpled cigarette.

I sit up, alarmed and surprised. "Flynn, what the hell do you think you're doing?"

He ignores me as he scans the room. "Where's that lighter we use to light candles with?" he asks.

"No, no, no." I wave my hands around as I jump up. But when he gives me a look to not go ballistic, to let this one slide, I sit back on the edge of the bed.

Giving up, I say, "The lighter's in the bathroom, next to the candle on the toilet tank lid."

"Thanks," he murmurs.

Flynn disappears to the bathroom, and less than a minute later, he reemerges with the cigarette, now lit, dangling from his lips. The tip glows an angry orangey-red in the dim lighting of the room.

"I'm only smoking this one, babe," Flynn assures me.

"Okay," I whisper, not convinced.

He walks over to the window in our room and starts fidgeting with the latch. "I promise, Jaynie. This is it."

"Flynn..." I shake my head. We have a thing about promises—

don't make ones today that you can't keep tomorrow.

When I open my eyes, Flynn has the bottom half of the window pushed open, though it's just a crack. Still, even that tiny bit is enough to allow the cool breeze to drift in. When winter's icy fingers reach me over on the bed, I'm filled with a sense of dread.

Flynn gestures that I should come over and sit next to him on the hardwood floor.

"Come on, Jaynie," he says softly. "I'll blow all the smoke out the window. We can even light some candles afterward to get rid of the smell. But, really"—his steel-gray eyes implore me to understand him on this one thing—"I need this smoke to calm my ass down."

"Why are you so on edge?" I ask, treading carefully. Sometimes it takes a little extra patience to get Flynn to talk. He's not like me. I always tell him everything. Well, unless not telling him is my only option.

"I want to come clean with you on what actually happened today over in Forsaken." He looks away. "The whole story, that is. Not just the part about the interview and running in to Crick. Those were good things."

"So…there is something bad."

He looks away. "Yes."

Folding my arms across my chest, I blow out a breath. "Damn it, Flynn, I knew there was more to this."

"Jaynie, just be quiet and get over here."

"But, it's cold," I murmur, resistant.

He reaches for a hoodie that's on the floor, some piece of clothing one of us discarded and never bothered to pick up. "Here," he says, "put this on. It'll keep you warm."

Before I give in and go to him—because I will, in fact, *always* go to Flynn—I say in a soft voice, "You went up there, didn't you? You went back to that goddamn place where we endured so much torment." My voice rises, as does my frustration. "You returned to the place where I lost my baby." I stifle a sob. "...the place where we lost *our* baby, Flynn."

"Jaynie, just come to me, please." His voice is a whisper, a comforting caress. God, I need him. He's the only person who can ever understand my pain, especially when it comes to this subject.

So I go to him.

And I let him slip the hoodie on me.

I then sit on the floor, across from him.

I also let him smoke his damn cigarette in peace.

Flicking an ash into a discarded paper cup, he tells me how after lunch, on a whim, he asked Crick to drive him up to the Lowry property.

"Why in the world would you ever want to go back up there?" I ask, truly perplexed.

"I don't know." He shrugs. "I just kind of wanted to see it today. That place where so much bad shit went down. It just seemed... I don't know..."

He's trying to explain, but this is clearly hard for him to put into words.

Flynn puts the cigarette to his lips and inhales, sucking smoke deeply into his lungs.

On his exhales, he says in a tight voice, "Hey, at least I didn't break any promises."

"What do you mean?"

"You hadn't yet asked me not to go up there. That didn't happen until tonight."

He has a point, so there's no good reason to dwell on promises that weren't technically broken. He went to the Lowry's and that's the end of it.

"So," I begin, curious to hear the rest of what happened up there. "You felt like you needed to see the place today...for whatever reason."

"Yeah, yeah, I did," he says, nodding.

"Why, though?" I press. "Why today of all days?"

He leans away from me and blows a puff of smoke out the open window. He then lowers the window a little when he sees me shivering.

"It's stupid, I know," he says, taking another drag. "Like you said, why today of all days? The whole time I lived in that fucking town, when we were apart, I avoided the Lowry property like it harbored the plague. But today, after getting the job, and after seeing Crick, I just felt like I needed closure or some shit."

In a small voice, I ask what I suspect may be the real reason Flynn was compelled to return to the Lowry property. "Did it have something to do with trying to heal?"

He looks down. "Maybe a little."

I nod, finally getting it, at least a little. Though I don't plan to ever return to that house of horrors, unless there's a damn good reason, I understand where Flynn's head was today.

See, he's not fully whole, either. And sometimes it's hard. Sometimes you need to revisit the past to spur yourself to the next step in your life. We all have different ways of dealing with grief. Flynn confronts it head-on, whereas I like to bury it.

"So," I breathe out. "What'd it look like?"

"What?" he asks. "The house?"

"Yeah, the house"—I make a sweeping motion with my hands—"but the rest of it too. How's the barn where we worked look? And what about all the surrounding land?"

"It all looks abandoned, Jaynie. Supposedly, the state owns *everything* now."

"Hmm, interesting," I remark.

The cigarette is down to little more than a butt. Flynn holds it like a joint and takes one last hit of nicotine.

Then he says, "They've seized *all* the property. That's what Crick told me. You should've seen it, though. There are all these big red

47

'No Trespassing' signs, posted everywhere you turn. They're on the trees lining the drive, on those huge gates out front…just all over the place."

He chuckles, and I ask, "What's so funny?"

"Eh, not funny like ha-ha. More like funny as in ironic."

"What's ironic?"

"Well, no one pays any attention to the signs. People still go up there."

"What do you mean?"

"Crick told me teens party up there all the time." An ash falls to the ground. "And it's kind of obvious. Remember that high wire fencing all around the perimeter, the one with barbed wire on top?"

"Like I could forget," I mutter, recalling our prison fencing all too clearly.

"Well, despite those signs to stay out, there are all these huge gaping holes in the fence that the partiers have created. I guess so they can get in more easily. Better than climbing, you know. That's what I kept thinking, anyway, when my ass was crawling through one of the bigger holes."

"Crick went with you, I hope?" I ask. "Please don't tell me you went in there all alone."

"I can take care of myself," Flynn assures me.

"Still…" I hate the idea of him up there all by himself. What if something had happened? "Where was Crick when you were deciding to trespass?" I add.

"He waited in the truck. I told him to keep guard in case someone showed up. You know, seeing as we weren't supposed to be up there snooping around in the first place. He'd told me earlier that the state cops have been stepping up patrols to keep the party crowd out."

"Well then, that was some good thinking on your part."

I smile over at Flynn, but he's busy staring out the window, out into the dark night.

"You should see it, Jaynie," he says, at last. "It's all fucked-up. The house is in pretty bad shape. Looks like midnight plumbers have hit it up a time or two...or ten."

Midnight plumbers are vandals who raid abandoned buildings for copper pipes and scrap metal to sell.

"I'm not surprised," I reply. "I'm sure there are plenty of pipes and stuff to rip off in that house."

Bad things happened there, but it was a nice house, aesthetically speaking.

Flynn nods. "Yeah, there's probably a lot of stuff of value in there. Or at least, there was. Anyway, after I checked out the house, I took a walk down to the work barn."

Mrs. Lowry ran a lucrative crafting business, built on the backs of the kids she fostered—like us—and funded on what we later discovered were embezzled funds. Flynn, Mandy, the twins, and me—we all spent long, arduous days working in that barn, which was really a kind of child-labor sweat shop.

"What was it like in the barn?" I whisper.

"Shit was destroyed," Flynn says. "Just like over in the house."

Smiling, I say, "Well, that's kind of poetic justice, now isn't it?"

Nodding, Flynn wets his fingers and presses together the tip of his cigarette. The cherry-red tip—though barely burning—hisses in protest. Setting the spent butt on the sill, he closes the window.

"It really is poetic justice," he agrees. "The barn, the house... Those places deserve to be destroyed, especially after all the shit that went down in them." His eyes meet mine, and he lowers his voice. "There was a table that was still standing upright in the work barn, one of those bench-style ones, where we used to sit for hours and hours, making those fucking crafts. Remember?"

"I'll *never* forget anything about that place, Flynn."

"Yeah, right, of course." He makes a face. "Anyway, I pushed that fucking table over till it was upside down, like a dead bug. Then I rolled it, like, five fucking times. I kicked it too. I just kept kicking it, Jaynie, over and over." He blows out a breath. "I hate to admit it, but knocking the shit out of that thing felt really good."

"I'm sure it did." I release a constrained breath of my own. "I kind of wish I'd been there to kick it a few times myself."

It's true. Though I don't care to return, the idea of fucking shit up in that place feels good.

"It was cathartic, no doubt," Flynn confirms.

"So what happened then? What made you so stressed out?"

Flynn stares over at the cigarette butt on the windowsill, eyeing it like he's wishing he had more.

Waving my hand toward the closet where he retrieved the first damn butt from his jacket, I say, "If you've got more, go get them. I'm sure a single night of smoking won't hook you back on the habit."

At that assertion, Flynn laughs.

"Yeah, actually it probably would hook me back. But it's okay. I don't have any more anyway. I bummed that one I had from Crick, right before we went our separate ways. I knew better than to buy a whole pack. That's why I went with the gum."

I'm relieved, but mostly I'm dying to know what has Flynn smoking again in the first place.

In a low voice, I ask, "What else happened up at there today?"

Sheepishly, eyes down, he says, "Uh, the cops showed up."

Chapter Nine

Flynn

"Oh shit, no way! You're kidding me, right?" Jaynie's face pales.

"Yeah, no… I mean…" I let out a groan and rub my hand down my face. "Yes, the cops showed up," I admit.

Jaynie is aghast.

"But, but, you *were* trespassing, Flynn. Are you in trouble now?" She pauses, surely considering all the possibilities, except the one she'll never guess. "Shit, please tell me you weren't arrested or fined?"

I let out a snort. "I'm here with you right now, aren't I?"

"Yeah, I guess. But maybe they took you in and released you. Maybe that's why you were so late."

"No, that was all the bus. And we may as well get used to that schedule, because that's the way it runs."

I'm stalling, and Jaynie knows it.

Eyeing me warily, she says, "Flynn, I don't care about the bus schedule. Damn it, what happened with the cops? Obviously something went down or you wouldn't have wanted a cigarette."

Chuckling at her fieriness, I assure her, "Nothing happened. At least, not in the way you're thinking. No arrests were made, no citations given. It wasn't like that at all."

Jaynie makes a grumpy face, stumped. "Then what was it like, Flynn? You, Crick, and the cops all go grab a coffee together or something?"

I better fess up. When Jaynie starts resorting to sarcasm, she's pissed.

And so I begin...

"Well, first off, there was only one cop in the car. And as it turns out, he's a detective."

"A detective...? Oh, ohhh..." Things begin to click for Jaynie, and she says, "He's investigating that missing girl case, right? The one Mandy told us about."

"He is," I confirm.

She gestures over to the nightstand. "Is that what you were trying to hide? That was his business card, wasn't it?"

"Yeah. His name is Detective Silver." I release a pent-up breath. It feels good to come clean. "Anyway, when he found out who I am, and, more importantly, my recent connection to our kind and caring Lowry friends"—I let out a sarcastic cough, and Jaynie grimaces—"he couldn't have cared less about me trespassing up there. Instead of the citation I was sure was coming, he gave me his business card."

"So he wants something from you?" Jaynie correctly guesses.

"Yeah, yeah, he does." I lean my head back against the wall and say, "He wanted to know if I'd be willing to help."

Skeptically, she says, "Help with what, exactly?"

I sure wish I had another smoke when I have to tell her, "He wants me to help with the missing girl case."

Carefully, voice level, Jaynie wants to know, "And in what way, *exactly*, does this detective think you can help?"

I lean forward and take both her hands in mine. We need

solidarity, now more than ever.

"Jaynie, Detective Silver thinks the body of the missing girl—her name was Debbie Canfield, by the way—may be buried somewhere up on the Lowry property. Maybe in the woods."

"Flynn," she counters, "the woods are endless. There are acres and acres of fields and forest. If that poor girl... Debbie, right?"—I nod—"Well, if this Debbie really is buried up there, she could be anywhere."

Our hands still intertwined, I squeeze and say, "Yeah, but think about it. If Allison or Mrs. Lowry—"

"You know it had to be Allison," Jaynie interjects. "Mrs. Lowry is wicked, but she's no killer."

She's probably right, as Allison *is* a sociopath.

I blow out a breath. "Okay. So if Allison murdered this Debbie girl, and we're looking at the event happening about seven years ago, she would've only been around fifteen at the time. Allison, that is," I clarify.

"A psycho even then," Jaynie murmurs.

"Yeah, well, psycho or not, she wouldn't have been strong enough to drag a body all the way up into the woods. And then, on top of that, dig a grave and bury said body."

"She disposed of that poor girl somewhere, Flynn."

"I know, I know. So hear me out."

Jaynie nods and I continue with my theory. "I think something happened. Probably down at the house... Or more likely in the work barn. Think about it, Jaynie. Those were the places where all our own altercations with Allison occurred."

She's quiet for a moment. Pondering, I guess.

At last, she says, "Yeah, but the barn where we worked wouldn't have been in existence back then. My social worker told me the day she dropped me off that *our* work barn was relatively new."

"Good point. And true, before our work barn was built, all the crafts were made up in the old barn."

Jaynie looks appalled. "You mean the one up on the hill? The one where we used to play freaking Hide and Seek with the twins?"

I nod grimly. "Yeah, that would be the one."

Letting go of my hands, Jaynie hangs her head. "God, Flynn. If that girl *is* buried up there, we probably tromped all over her grave dozens of times."

"Hey, we don't know if she's buried there." I try to sound reassuring. "In fact, we don't know anything yet. But even if it turns out to be true, how could we have known?"

"I guess," Jaynie grudgingly concedes. And then she asks, "Did you tell the detective all of this?"

"No, not yet."

"Wait, why not? I thought he wanted your help with the case."

"He does, but he wants more than guesses and theories. He wants me to do some kind of an official walk-through on the property with him. That way I can point out *all* the places I think Allison could've buried a body. The old barn's the most likely place, seeing as it was *the* work barn when she was there. But, I don't know, I could be wrong."

"So," Jaynie says on a loud sigh. "You're completely set on doing this, aren't you? Even if it means spending more time in a place we both hate."

I think it over carefully before I respond. But, really, I have no choice but to say. "If it helps keep Allison behind bars—and, more importantly, away from you—I'll sleep up in that damn place if they need me to."

"You will do no such thing, Flynn O'Neill."

"Okay. But I'm going to help, Jaynie. In any way I can."

She just about blows me away when she then declares, "Well, you're not doing this alone. If you're going to help with the case, then damn it, so am I."

Chapter Ten

Jaynie

Flynn's busy working his new job all week, and I continue with my own shifts at the sandwich shop. We're too tired most nights to discuss much of anything, let alone the case of the missing girl and how we're supposed to help. Sometimes I can't believe I volunteered to return to the Lowry house, considering all my misgivings. But something deep inside my heart compelled me to offer my assistance.

Doing so has been good for me too, in a surprising way. Taking the reins and feeling in control is something I've missed. Not that I've had tons of experience knowing how these things feel.

But I'm learning. And it's making me feel, dare I say, empowered.

I've noticed my nightmares have lessened this week, and that's a first. In addition, I'm not hoarding as many candy bars as before. Hopefully, this positive progress will continue. I just pray I don't lose my shit when I actually step back on the Lowry property.

I'll have to keep reminding myself, again and again, that Flynn is there with me so I'll be okay.

It seems so distant anyway.

But then it happens—Flynn calls Detective Silver on Friday evening, and the proverbial ball starts rolling.

Placing the detective on speaker, Flynn first informs him that I will be joining their effort to try and locate the burial spot for the unfortunate Debbie Canfield. To say Detective Silver is pleased to have two of us onboard would be an understatement.

He gushes to Flynn, "That's great. Another set of eyes can only help, especially eyes belonging to someone who once lived up there too."

They talk a bit more, and I sort of zone out, until I hear Detective Silver asking if we can meet him tomorrow.

Whoa, that soon? I think, panicked.

"Sure," Flynn says. "That works for us."

"Great," I murmur sarcastically, and Flynn's gaze snaps to me.

He quickly wraps up with Detective Silver, and, turning to me, says, "You can always back out, Jaynie."

"No, I'm good," I insist.

But really, am I?

Sleep eludes me that night. Well, that's no surprise, considering. In any case, I end up waking Flynn with all my tossing and turning.

He kisses the top of my head and pulls me to him. In a sleepy voice, he murmurs, "Let's call the detective in the morning and cancel. Let's see if we can meet him another time. Or I could always go alone tomorrow."

"No." I snuggle in closer to this guy who has the ability to soothe my troubled self. "I should be fine," I continue, "as long as you're there with me."

"Always," Flynn whispers. "I'll always be by your side, Jaynie. For all the simple things and for all this harder stuff too."

"I don't deserve you," I whisper.

But Flynn silences my insecurity with kisses. Lots of kisses.

Things proceed to heat up quickly, as they always do, and soon all sleep clothes are discarded. We then find things to do—such as giving each other intense pleasure—to keep apprehension at bay.

The next morning, however, my nerves are back on edge.

As we ride on a bus bound for Forsaken, I'm as jittery as ever.

"Now I understand why you needed a cigarette the other night," I joke to Flynn. I laugh shakily, my knees bouncing up and down, a motion I find oddly soothing. "I've never smoked, but maybe I should start."

I'm kidding, but Flynn doesn't find my statement amusing.

"Don't ever start," he warns. "Once you're hooked, it's hard to ever quit completely. You always have those cravings."

"I was only joking," I assure him, my knees moving faster.

"I know, babe." Flynn places his hand on one leg and calms the movement of both. "Keep it together, Jaynie. You got this," he tells me. "Everything will go smoothly."

When his hand remains on my leg, I note, "You're really warm, Flynn."

He squeezes my thigh, which is covered by a thin pair of black leggings. "Yeah, good call on your part, wearing lighter clothes." He nods down to the heavy winter parka he's wearing. "Me? I don't know what I was thinking. I'm dying in this heavy coat. It's making me hot as hell."

"You *are* hot as hell." I wink as I nudge his shoulder.

Chuckling, Flynn lowers his head, embarrassed. "Jaynie..."

I adore how sometimes he's suddenly shy about his good looks. It makes him all the more attractive.

But I do feel for him on the coat thing. Neither of us bothered to check the weather; I just lucked out. It's still early spring, but this March day seems to be warming up rapidly. I grabbed a jacket before we left, but mine is much lighter than Flynn's. I have on a worn, threadbare hand-me-down I snatched at a local thrift store last month.

"You should just leave your coat in Detective Silver's car once we're up at the house," I suggest. "It'll be too hot walking around the Lowry property wearing that thing."

"Yeah," he mumbles, suddenly distracted.

I realize then that we're nearing the bus stop. And Flynn is nervous too. Facing your demons head-on, the ones from the past, that crap's never easy. But we can do this. We made a promise to assist the detective and now we're committed to following through.

I review the plan in my head, trying to look at things objectively.

We meet Detective Silver at the bus stop, where he'll drive us up to the Lowry place. From there we'll conduct what the detective termed a 'walk-through,' throughout which he'd like for us to give him any info we deem useful in finding the missing girl's remains.

And now there's no more time to think.

For better or worse, it's show-time...

When we reach the stop, the lumbering bus slows to a crawl, and then comes to a complete stop. Flynn taps the fingerprint-smudged window to draw my attention to a nondescript white sedan parked at the curb. Though the vehicle is unmarked, it's clear it's a law enforcement car.

"There's our ride," Flynn confirms. "That's Detective Silver's car."

"Here goes nothing," I mutter.

I'm apprehensive about meeting new people, especially those in positions of power. But Detective Silver turns out to be really nice. He puts me at ease almost immediately with his warm, affable ways.

While he makes small talk with Flynn, I look him over. He must be in his early forties. Not a bad-looking man, the detective's tall and thin, with salt-and-pepper hair that's thick and neatly coifed.

As we stand on the sidewalk, I start to feel uneasy, though. For some reason, the detective's attention has focused more and more on me. After a few minutes, he's eyeing me intently, his pale blue eyes assessing.

So much for putting me at ease.

"Okayyy," I mutter under my breath as I shift from one sneakered foot to the other.

When the detective frowns, his gaze never wavering from me, Flynn, who's obviously as curious as I am as to what could be so utterly fascinating about me, clears his throat and flat-out asks the detective, "Sir, is there something wrong with Jaynie? You keep looking at her like something's really wrong."

"Oh, no, nothing is wrong." The detective, averting his gaze, rubs a hand down his face. "And I do apologize."

He's clearly embarrassed, and after a long pause, his eyes return to me, albeit in an apologetic manner.

"Again," he says, "let me reiterate that I'm sorry for staring at you like that, Miss Cumberland. It's just that you look remarkably similar to the missing girl, Debbie Canfield."

Immediately disturbed by this revelation, I say, "You're kidding, right?"

"I'm afraid I'm not," the detective grimly replies.

"Oh, wonderful," I say, my voice high and laced with sarcasm. "I look like the girl who went missing. Are you sure about this?"

"Here, let me show you." Detective Silver fishes what looks to be a small color photograph of Debbie Canfield from the pocket of his trench coat. He hands me it to me. And crap. Sixteen-year-old Debbie, to my dismay, looks an awful lot like me.

"Oh, wow," I murmur as I stare down at the photo.

The resemblance is truly uncanny. I am older, of course—eighteen, not sixteen. But otherwise we look a lot alike. Debbie has the same wavy auburn hair, similar green eyes, and high cheekbones, just like me.

"Holy shit," Flynn exclaims when I pass the picture over for him to take a look.

He quickly hands the photo back to the detective, like it's too difficult for him to peer down at a girl who so closely resembles me. And one who is currently presumed to be dead.

Shit, I kind of feel the same way.

"Maybe this explains why Allison hated me so much right from the start," I offer, shuddering. "If she's the one who did do something to Debbie, then when I showed up, looking so similar to the girl she'd offed, it had to have been disturbing to her."

"To say the least," Flynn mumbles.

The detective pulls a notepad from his coat and starts asking questions. "Do you feel you were singled out during your time at the Lowry residence? Were you treated more harshly than the others, particularly at the hand of Allison Lowry?"

I glance over at Flynn. He takes my hand, offering his support for whatever I choose to do. Truth is, though, I don't really care to share the horrible things that were done to me, not with the detective...or anyone else.

"We all had it bad," I whisper, head bowed.

"Miss Cumberland, even if we don't find the body of the missing girl, you could help build a case against Ms. Lowry. There's a good chance she'd remain in prison longer than what she's currently looking at if she were charged with assault."

My head jerks up. "Does that mean you have some insight regarding her sentence? Flynn and I calculated that the earliest she'd be up for parole is sometime next year."

Detective Silver shoots me an apologetic look. "That would be true under normal circumstances," he begins, sighing. "But I'm afraid with the overcrowding situation as it is at the women's correction facility where Allison resides, and also with her being in for a non-violent offense, there's a better-than-good chance she'll be up for early release *this* summer."

"*This* summer? That's only a few months away." There's real fear in my tone when I turn to Flynn and say, "We should move to another state."

I am terrified of Allison, but thankfully Flynn sees things more rationally than I.

"Jaynie," he says, "we're not letting Allison chase us away, not again. We ran once, but at least we ended up where we always planned to go. We have connections here in West Virginia. Mandy and the twins are up in Morgantown, and Bill Delmont is in Lawrence. Hell, even here in Forsaken, I have a friend in Crick."

"But—"

"No, Jaynie. We need our support system. Plus, I just landed a decent-paying job. You still have your position at the sandwich shop, and I can pick up a shift there when things get busy. More money will be coming in real soon. We can buy a car, find a better apartment, all those things we talked about. If we run, we'll have to start all over again."

Everything Flynn says is making sense.

But there's still a part of me that longs to flee.

"Hold up," Detective Silver interjects. "There's no need for Jaynie to put anything on record today." He slips the notepad back in his pocket and gestures to his car. "Let's take that ride up to the property. We'll simply look around the place like we planned."

"Sounds good to me," I say.

"Yeah, fine," Flynn echoes.

But when we slip into the back of the detective's car, Flynn hesitates midway across the seat and I end up smooshed up against his side. I have a perfect view of what's delayed him when he carefully lifts a docket of files and two vials of what looks to be blood up from the seat.

When he starts to move the items from the seat to the floor, Detective Silver stops him. "Oh, hey," he says, grabbing the stuff. "I'll take care of that."

The detective then opens the driver's door and slides the file and the vials of blood over to the empty seat next to him.

"Are those the files on Debbie Canfield?" Flynn asks.

"Yes," Detective Silver replies as he puts on his seat belt.

"And those vials..." Flynn's eyes meet the detective's in the rearview mirror. "Is that the missing girl's blood?"

The detective nods. "Yes, it is. We were lucky to secure two blood samples from Debbie Canfield's time under state's care. Those were never disposed of, and that's very fortunate for us. We're going to need her blood for a DNA match. That is, if we ever come across any evidence up on the Lowry property."

The blood from the missing girl makes this endeavor feel so real. I shudder and Flynn takes my hand. "You sure you're up for doing this?" he asks softly, so the detective can't hear. "We can still tell him no. You could always wait here in town while I ride up with him. We could meet up after we're done."

I'm immediately relieved at the prospect of an out, but the truth remains that I need to face my fears. Burying the past hasn't been working. Though not as frequent as in the beginning, my nightmares continue. And I can't stop hoarding food, not completely. Things have improved this week, yes, mainly because I'm facing this crap head-on. So, really, why would I give up now? Bottom line, I can't back out.

"No," I tell Flynn. "I'm coming along. I *need* to do this with you."

I don't add that if we get through today, there's something else I'd like to do. I'm hoping I'll find the courage to talk about my experiences with Allison, and ultimately help Detective Silver build an assault case against her.

Because if there's one thing I have no doubt of, it's that that bitch needs to stay behind bars.

Chapter Eleven

Flynn

Finding my sorry ass back on the Lowry property is no easier than it was the first go-round. However, it's not me I'm worried about on this day. It's Jaynie who concerns me. She had it a whole lot worse than any of us during her time here, especially towards the end.

That's why I feel the need to keep checking to make sure she's all right.

"Do you want to turn around?" I ask as we walk with Detective Silver to the brick colonial house we once called home. I've been noticing her glancing longingly back at the car, so this seems like a good time to ask if she still wants to do this. "Jaynie, we can leave. Right now, if that's what you want."

"No." She squeezes my hand. "I'm still good."

I wonder though, as her hand has remained locked with mine since the car ride up. Her skin usually feels cool, and her grasp is light and easy. But not today. Today she's sweating bullets and holding on to me for dear life.

When we reach the house, Detective Silver declares, "I'd like for us to begin the walk-through inside."

"I really think the old barn would be a better place to start," I counter.

"We'll get there, Flynn," Detective Silver assures me. "But first I'd like to hit these buildings one by one."

"Okay," I say as I watch Jaynie nod her assent.

On our way up to the porch that's attached to the front of the house, we're careful to watch our step. The walkway is crumbling and it'd be easy to trip. Wow, everything looks so different. Even the flowers that once lined the sides of the stone path are long gone. The porch, as we begin to climb the steps, has so many gaping holes marking the floorboards that we have to step around them in a zig-zag pattern.

"This place is a mess," Jaynie murmurs when we reach the door. The front door that is, as the screen door, ripped from its hinges, is lying off to the side.

"Yes, conditions up here are bad," Detective Silver says. "Be sure to tread lightly and watch that you don't step on any sharp objects once we're in the house."

In the house, when Jaynie gasps upon viewing the appearance, I lean in and whisper, "I told you the place looked like it'd been hit by a tornado."

And it has. The furniture that wasn't outright stolen has been knocked all over, busted into pieces in most cases. Whole sections of the hardwood floors have been ripped up, and there are holes punched into the walls. Frayed wires and busted pipes jut out, appearing almost lewd with their obscene angles.

"Ugh, this is gross. Looks like some partiers really went to town in here," Jaynie remarks as she steps over a pile of empty beer cans and used condoms.

Detective Silver, getting down to the business of why we're here, asks if we happen to remember any hiding places in the house. "I'm hoping being back here may spur some memories," he says, a statement that makes Jaynie wince. Stirred memories are the last thing my girl needs.

"Nothing comes to mind," I'm quick to say.

"Think about places where a body could be stowed away," he goes on. "Any small cubby holes or secret passages could harbor more than just dust."

"Secret passages?" I mumble. "This place isn't that extensive."

"Besides," Jaynie adds, "If there'd been a secret passageway, we certainly would've used it to escape."

"Yeah," I agree. And then I add, "Wouldn't you think if a body was buried in the house we would have noticed a smell."

Jaynie scrunches up her nose. "Flynn," she chastises. "That's disgusting."

"It's also highly doubtful," the detective chimes in. "Debbie Canfield disappeared a few years before you or Jaynie lived here. If a body had ever been hidden in this house, it would've likely been nothing but bones by the time you got here."

Jaynie, shuddering, says, "Okay, okay. I still don't think the body was ever in this house. I mean, look around." She gestures to the mess about us. "If a body was hidden *anywhere* in this place, even if it was now nothing but a skeleton, someone surely would have found it by now."

"That's a valid point," the detective agrees as he scans the debris.

"My money's still on the old barn up in the fields," I interject.

Detective Silver turns to me. "Yes, you seem so certain that this old barn will hold something. But I wanted to ask you a question before we head up there."

"Sure, shoot."

"Don't you think the newer structure would be a better place to search?" Detective Silver motions to where the work barn, the pole barn where we once made crafts, is located, down a slope just beyond the house. "That newer barn is much closer to this place," the detective goes on. "And that would've made it that much easier for an assailant to transport a body, assuming the murder took place in here. That barn outside was the official workplace, correct?"

I shake my head as I say, "It was *our* work barn, yes, but that wasn't where the kids made crafts back when Debbie lived here."

"What do you mean?" the detective asks.

"The barn where we worked, the one you're talking about, is relatively new. But the old barn…" I point to an intact window, one with a view up the hill from the house. "See that old structure up there? That's where Debbie would've worked. That's the barn I have a feeling about. That's the one we should be searching."

"It makes the most sense to me too," Jaynie says, jumping in. "Even though the old barn used to be the work area at one time, not too many people spent any time up there after the new barn was finished. That made it remote and private."

"Interesting," Detective Silver muses. And then he asks, "Have either of you ever been inside that structure?"

Jaynie takes the lead in responding to this question, which I welcome. It means she's growing more comfortable with being back here.

"We would venture up there from time to time," she tells Silver. "I actually think we were the first kids to play up there in ages. Still, we kept mostly to the outside area. If we did venture into the barn, it was never for more than a minute or two. See, it's really dark and kind of creepy in there."

Detective Silver states grimly, "I think we better take a look inside this old barn."

Retracing our steps over the same fields Jaynie and I ran through our final and desperate night brings up a myriad of emotions. I'm usually good at keeping my feelings bottled up, especially in front of strangers, but this time is different. Those stirred-up emotions get the best of me, and I have to stop for a minute to get a hold of myself.

Bending over and placing my hands on my knees, Jaynie touches my shoulder lightly. "Flynn, are you all right?"

"Yeah, sure, I'm good. Just a little overheated is all."

I make a production of fanning myself, but Jaynie knows I'm full of shit. I mean, come on. I left my heavy coat in the detective's car because I was too warm. But it's not really all *that* warm today, not when you're wearing a light T-shirt like I am. Plus there's the fact that I'm in really good shape. Trekking up a hill would hardly result in me sucking wind and complaining of the heat.

Still, my girl has my back and plays along. That's what we do—we cover for each other, always.

"Go ahead and rest up for a minute," Detective Silver says when Jaynie asks if we can have a minute for me to cool down. "I have a quick call I need to make, anyway."

When he's a good distance from us, I turn to Jaynie and say, "I think he's onto us. He's no dummy. He knows I'm not overheated. I bet he doesn't even need to make a call."

"Maybe not," she says softly. "Maybe he's just being nice. I think it's possible. I really do get a good vibe from him."

I nod. "Yeah, I do too. That's why I agreed to help in the first place. And, as for you, I could tell you were okay with him when you jumped in the conversation down at the house."

"I *am* okay with him," she confirms. "And aside from him being a decent human being, I think he really does want to solve this case."

"I think he does too," I agree.

"It's only right, Flynn. If that poor girl Debbie really is buried up here, she deserves justice."

"Yeah..." I run a hand through my scruffy hair as I smile over at Jaynie. "She definitely does."

I love that she is so amped to help. Maybe helping people, even people who are no longer with us, is what she needs to heal.

Peering up at the barn, the rotted wood exterior appearing dark and wet, she says, "So you definitely think that barn is the most likely place for Debbie to have been buried?"

"Well, I don't know for sure," I reply. "But yeah, the old barn is where I'd start."

Her brow creasing, like it does when she's worried, Jaynie asks, "What if she's *not* in the barn, though? What then, Flynn? What if the police can't find a body up on this property *anywhere*?"

Jaynie makes a sweeping motion to the acres and acres of fields and forest surrounding us, and I mumble, "It is a daunting task."

I take it all in for another minute, and finally I say, "I don't know, babe, but I hope like hell that the girl *is* buried in the old barn. Otherwise, she'll probably never be found."

Jaynie makes a face, a very unhappy face. Her enthusiasm seems to be waning.

In a dull tone, she says, "If that happens, then Allison will be released from prison for sure, Flynn. Possibly as early as this summer."

"Fuck."

I wave the detective back over and gesture to the barn, which is only a short distance from where we're stopped. "Hey, look," I say. "I'm good now. Let's go search that goddamn barn for hiding spots."

"Okay," he says. "Let's go."

Christ, it's imperative that we find that body, now more than ever. Because now there are two reasons, at least for me. 1) I need Allison to stay in prison. And 2) I need to keep Jaynie safe, physically *and* emotionally.

Well, she doesn't know it, but if we fail today I may just have a backup plan.

Of course, it's a plan I hope to never have to resort to.

Chapter Twelve

Jaynie

*Y*ep, the barn is as creepy as ever, all dark and musty-smelling. Water is dripping from various places, the result of a dilapidated roof. This structure is definitely an unpleasant place in which to walk around.

But walk around, we must.

"I can't believe Mandy was brave enough to come in here on her own last year to search for candles for the twin's birthday," I muse as I step over a fallen rafter.

"She told me she was quick about it," Flynn, following behind me, replies.

"I bet she was."

"Don't worry. It shouldn't take us too long to go through this place," he says reassuringly. "It's not that large."

Flynn is trying, like always, to make me feel better about what we have to do. But the truth is we can't simply race in and out. We made a promise to Detective Silver to help conduct a *thorough* search. And that, unfortunately, is going to require more than a few minutes of traipsing around, looking to and fro.

The detective already told us that first off the entire dirt floor needs to be examined for uneven places. That could indicate an old burial location. Next, there are stalls to check around in. Plus, there's a few old trunks strewn about that need searching.

One of those old relics is probably where Mandy found those birthday candles.

It's then that I notice a lid on one of the trunks is not completely closed. Shiny holiday items, various colors of tinsel and a homemade foil star, are spilling out through the opening.

Flynn, following my gaze, says, "Detective Silver said we need to go through all those old trunks."

"Yeah, I heard him, but I really don't know why," I counter. "They're too small to hold a body." I motion to the trunk with the tinsel and star. "See, it's all holiday stuff."

"I know. But he thinks there could be a weapon, or something relevant, stowed away in all that junk. Or..." He looks away, then mumbles, "Never mind."

"Wait." I grab his arm. "What were you going to say?"

Sighing, he says, "He mentioned that Allison could've cut up the body and tossed the pieces in a trunk."

"Ugh! Flynn, that's a hideous thought."

He shrugs. "If the girl was killed, then it was obviously a hideous crime. What do you expect, Jaynie?"

"I don't know. Just...not that."

"If you ask me, this whole task is disgusting."

He's not wrong about that.

"Okay, Flynn and Jaynie." The detective, thankfully, comes over and interrupts our unpleasant discussion. "Let's get to work."

He and Flynn start by canvassing the dirt floor, while I am assigned to go through the musty, old trunks.

Thankfully, I find no body parts.

Aside from some other antiquated holiday decorations, I come upon nothing more than a few ratty blankets and a bunch of old tools.

"Nothing of interest in any of these," I announce when I'm finished.

"We should check up in the hayloft," Flynn suggests.

He and the detective have just finished with the barn floor, so up the old rickety ladder the three of us go, with the detective in the lead.

In the hayloft, there's nothing to be found besides mountains of dust.

After a succession of sneezes, I clear my throat and ask, "Where to now?"

"Let's go back down the ladder," the detective says.

"Works for me," Flynn replies, suppressing a sneeze of his own.

Back in the base of the barn, we look around one last time, hoping to find something we missed.

But when it's clear there's nothing more to search, Flynn says, "That's it, I guess. There's nothing left for us to do. There are no other areas to search. We covered everything in here."

Sighing, I dejectedly add, "I don't think there are any bodies buried in this barn."

Rubbing the salt-and-pepper stubble on his chin, Detective Silver blows out a breath. "You may be right," he says. "But then again…" He digs the toe of his shiny dress shoe into the dirt floor, creating a divot. "Maybe our victim is buried below where we're standing."

"Uh, we just canvassed the whole floor," Flynn reminds him. "You said yourself there's no indication anyone's dug around in this old barn in years."

"Yes, but the body could be buried much deeper. If the killer—"

"Allison, you mean," I mutter.

"—took it upon him- or herself to rake the dirt every day, after a while any sign of a disturbance would have been whisked away."

"Gross." The detective sure has a colorful—and vivid—way of explaining things.

Flynn, obviously eager to see this case resolved for my sake, says, "Should we grab some shovels?"

Detective Silver thumps him on the back. "No, son, I think you and Jaynie have done enough for the day. Though it's generous of you to offer, I believe this is a job best suited for our excavation crew. I was hoping we'd have more luck today, but all in all I think we did well. I appreciate you two coming in to town to help. The authorities can take it from here on out."

Panicked that this is our last chance to keep Allison behind bars, and it's slipping from our grasp, I hastily inquire, "You'll keep us updated on any and all progress, right?"

"Sure, sure, I can do that." The detective shares a meaningful glance with me alone. "Of course, there's always the option of you telling your own story, Jaynie. Especially if we don't find anything after the excavation is complete."

"Does that mean Allison is off the hook if you come up empty-handed?" I inquire.

"No body and no evidence equal no case, I'm afraid." The detective peers at me, kindness in his blue eyes. "Think about making a statement, okay? Think of it as a backup plan, if nothing else."

I know people, including this man, only want to see me receive the justice I deserve. But the thought of making an official statement and, worse yet, having to testify in court—telling my story to complete strangers—is something I prefer to avoid.

"I don't know," I whisper. "Maybe."

"Hey," Flynn says, jumping to my defense. "Can she think about it for a while?"

"Yes, of course. Let's see what comes from the excavation before any decisions have to be made."

"Can't you just excavate the whole place?" I ask. "Like, why not tear down the house, dig up all the fields, check everywhere for the body of that girl?"

"I wish we could." Detective Silver's tone is apologetic. "But without probable cause, there's no way a judge will ever approve something as extreme as that. The cost factor alone is prohibitive. That's why I *needed* you to come to the property today. Now, because of your assistance, I can justify a more thorough search. At least, one of this old barn. But beyond that…"

"We're fucked," Flynn finishes for him.

Chapter Thirteen

Flynn

Days pass, and the next thing I know it's been a whole week since our search of the barn.

Even so, Jaynie and I hear nothing from Detective Silver. There are no updates at all regarding the excavation. And that's frustrating as hell.

Fed up with waiting, one afternoon when work lets out early, I decide to go up to the Lowry property and check on shit for myself. Since I don't have a car, though, that involves giving Crick a call to ask him for a helping hand.

"Whatcha up to, kid?" my old friend inquires when I hit him up.

"Not much," I reply. "How's shit with you?"

We proceed to shoot the breeze for a minute or two, until I finally get around to asking, "Hey, any chance you have time to drive me up to the old Lowry property today?"

"You just can't stay away from that place, can you, my friend?" Crick replies. I envision him shaking his head, perplexed by my fascination with a home that brought me so much misery.

"It's not that," I insist. "I just need to, uh, check on something."

Crick agrees to help. The best part is he doesn't ask questions; he just picks me up out at the jobsite and drives me up to the old Lowry homestead.

We actually don't do much talking at all on the way there. We're comfortable enough with one another to handle the silence. Plus, with all I've got on my mind, I'm good with keeping the chatter to a minimum.

When we reach our destination, I hop out of Crick's truck. Striding to the front gate, I shade my eyes from the glare of the setting sun.

Through the wire fence, I peer down at my once-upon-a-time home. "And a crappy home it was," I murmur, feeling like the world is against us, once more.

But then I spy heavy construction equipment, parked up by the house, and my mood is lifted. "Thank Christ," I mumble.

Shit, I still have so many trust issues. Even though I truly believe he's a good guy, a part of me didn't fully believe Detective Silver. Especially since I haven't heard from him since the day we were up here. That's why I felt so compelled to come back today, to see if he'd kept his word.

Once I'm back in the truck, Crick, sensing my better mood, finally gets around to asking me why I was so amped to come up to the Lowry property today. Since I trust Crick—he's one of the few people I do trust besides Jaynie—I quietly share with him the details of the missing girl case.

Leaning back as I finish my tale, Crick lets out a low whistle. "Shit," he says, rubbing his forehead with his hand. "I used to hear the rumors about what was going on up at this place. You know, all the child labor shit and whatnot."

He shoots me a *mea culpa* sidelong glance, and though it's not necessary, I do appreciate the sentiment. "Thanks," I murmur.

"Anyway," he continues, "I'll tell you one thing."

"What's that, Crick?"

"I sure feel bad now. Fessing up to the fact that I never really put much stock into all that talk makes me feel lower than garbage. It's just that I never thought about it much. Not till I met you, and you started telling me how fucked-up things were for you and the other kids who lived here. It was too late by then, though. The place had already been shut down."

"Crick..." I blow out a breath. "There's no reason in the world for you to feel bad."

"No crying over spilled pop, yeah?"

I don't correct him that he probably means 'spilled milk.' I just simply say, "There was nothing you or anyone else could have done, not really. Before she went to prison, Mrs. Lowry was looked upon as a godsend to this town. The state foster care system sure saw her in that light, that's for sure."

"Still, kid... If a girl lost her life up here... Well, shit, man. Let's just say it doesn't leave me feelin' too good about myself for blowing off those rumors."

Crick appears truly stricken. But there's no sense in him suffering too. Mrs. Lowry and Allison have hurt enough fucking people.

I focus on what's really important and say, "Hey, at least something's being done about it now."

"Better late than ever, I guess."

Chuckling, I do correct him on that one, if only to simply lighten the mood. "I think the phrase goes 'better late than *never*.'"

Crick starts up his truck. "Yeah. That too, kid," he replies.

*B*ack at the apartment, I give Jaynie the update.

"So there's definitely excavation equipment up there?" she

inquires, double-checking.

I shake my head. Jaynie is as distrustful as I am. Maybe someday we'll get past this since it'd sure feel good to take people at their word.

"Flynn?" she prompts.

To which I assure her, "Yes, there's equipment there…lots of it. Detective Silver kept his promise to us."

We're both relieved.

But the waiting game continues.

While we await word of any progress, good or bad, Jaynie and I try to get on with our lives. And, after a while, something interesting begins to happen—life starts to become, well, kind of normal.

Jaynie mentions exactly that one afternoon, and I say, "Normal is good, babe. We need normal."

Our days soon take on a comforting routine, one in which we find a tiny thread of solace. And that's good. We can work with a thread. A thread leads to two, then three. Soon enough, that happens and we start sewing together the normal pieces of a life we've never known.

We build something.

We work and we love and we play.

And we heal more and more.

We learn to have fun again, finding joy in even the smallest of things.

An example…

One Friday afternoon, a light snow begins to fall. By four o'clock, it's blizzard-time. When the bus drops me off around seven, there must be six inches on the ground, maybe more. Lawrence is a ghost town, but I kind of like it.

After trudging down a slippery sidewalk, thankful that I have on my heaviest of work boots, I tromp into the sandwich shop.

Jaynie is closing out the cash register and yells up to me, "Take off your boots!"

Chuckling, I do as she asks, and then I pad to the back in my wooly socks.

There's not a single customer in the shop, so I'm not the least bit surprised when Jaynie looks up from the register and informs me, "Bill went home early because of all the snow. He told me to go ahead and close up. No one is coming out in this mess."

"Not likely," I reply, yawning as I take a seat on a stool.

"You want some coffee?" she asks.

I take off my gloves. "Yeah, sure. That'd be great, babe."

Jaynie finishes with the register, pours me some coffee, and then starts wrapping up cold cuts and cheeses she pulls from a case under the counter.

"You want any help putting that stuff away?" I ask.

"Yeah"—she pushes a roll of salami and two cheeses my way—"sure."

My stomach starts to growl, which makes Jaynie smack her head and declare, "Crap. I forgot all about dinner."

"I am kind of famished," I state. "Lunch was hours ago. I'm probably pretty close to starving about now."

I'm teasing around, but I realize my mistake immediately when Jaynie's eyes meet mine. "You're just kidding, right?" She chews at her bottom lip. "You're just a normal kind of hungry, I hope?"

Despite making progress, there are still days, for both of us, when no amount of food is enough. But today I'm okay, and I assure Jaynie, "I'm just regular hungry. It was a bad joke on my part."

She breathes a sigh of relief. And then there's this moment of stilted silence, where I meticulously wrap up Swiss cheese and she fidgets with a stack of plates, straightening them all in until they're in an even pile.

Reminders of the past, and the fact we've not yet erased our demons, always tend to dampen our moods.

But Jaynie seems determined to keep us forward-focused, when, in a cheery tone, she says, "Speaking of dinner, I can easily throw some ham and cheese sandwiches together. We can even press them into paninis if you want."

I smile at her. "Yeah, that sounds like fun."

She continues. "There's also some leftover potato salad. We can finish that off too. I doubt it'll stay good for much longer."

"Works for me," I reply.

Part of our rental agreement with Bill is that we're allowed to eat anything we want from the sandwich shop. It works out nicely too, since we have no kitchen up in our room. Yet another reason why we need a larger apartment.

All in due time. A car comes first.

After pressing paninis and polishing off two sandwiches each, along with that soon-to-expire potato salad—which actually tastes perfectly fresh to me—Jaynie and I move to the front of the store so we can watch the snow fall outside the big picture window facing the street.

We settle into one of the plushiest sofas, and nestling back against me, her auburn hair fanning out across my chest, Jaynie says, "It really is beautiful, Flynn."

She means the snow, but I only have eyes for her.

Reaching down to lift a strand of her shiny hair, I hold it up to the light. As I admire all the shimmery hues of copper, I murmur, "Yes, definitely beautiful."

She twists around to face me, her hair falling from my grasp like a liquefied precious metal. "I meant the snow, silly," she says with a chuckle.

Urging her to lay face-down against me, I wrap my arms around her back. "I knew what you meant," I say lightly. "But as pretty as the snow is I'd much rather look at you. You're far more gorgeous."

To me, that's the God's-honest truth. A lot of guys would serve up lines like that, well, as lines. But corny as it sounds I genuinely feel that way about Jaynie. I see the purest of beauty when I look at her.

"Flynn, Flynn, Flynn…" She rests her cheek against my chest, her fingers sliding beneath the hem of my shirt. A move made simply to give us more of the skin-to-skin contact we never stop craving. "Did I tell you I love you yet today?"

"Maybe this morning," I reply. "But tell me again. I never get tired of hearing it."

"I love you," she says.

Three simple words composed of three syllables. How amazing it never ceases to be when I hear them pass Jaynie's lips. Those words hold the power to lift me up, to soothe my soul, and to make me a better man.

And that's what Jaynie deserves—the best me that I can be.

Chapter Fourteen

Jaynie

*I*t takes some fancy talking, but I finally succeed in convincing Flynn that we should ditch the sandwich shop for a couple hours and go out and play in the snow.

"Are you crazy?" he says initially. "I walked from the bus stop, remember? It's not only a pain to get around in all that snow, but it's freaking cold as hell out there."

"Oh, come on." I tug at him, urging him up from the sofa. "Live a little. We can wear lots of layers. And besides, it's April. This is probably the last big snow till next year."

"How can I argue with reasoning like that," he then says.

Fifteen minutes later, bundled up and ready for the Arctic, we find ourselves outside in a wintry wonderland. The snow still falls, fast and furious, but we're making the most of it. No traffic in the streets means we're able to start an impromptu snowball fight, right outside the front of the shop.

I get in a few nice hits right away, then I zigzag my way across the road to the other side. When Flynn proceeds to lob a succession of icy white balls my way, I run around the side of the building and make a getaway.

My plan is to flee to the nearby park.

"Hey, no fair," I hear him calling out to me as I run off, his voice fading as I break into a sprint. "You're way out of firing range."

"You're damn right I am," I holler back.

I don't know if he hears me, but I pick up speed, just in case he's gaining on me. It's hard to see with all the falling snow.

Sure enough, Flynn, who is far faster than I am, catches up to me in no time, just as I'm about to enter the park.

Giving up hope that I can escape him—at least for the moment—I spin around and fall into his arms. "Okay, you win," I say, breathless, as I peer up at him.

Chuckling, he nods to the woodsy entrance. "You still want to play in the park?"

"Yeah,"—I nod—"sure."

Leaning down like he's about to whisper some sweet nothing in my ear, he murmurs, "I call for a rematch in the park. And maybe, if I'm feeling generous, I'll let you win this time."

"Oh, really?" I twist out of his grasp and bump his hip with mine. "I see how you are. You think I can't win against you fairly. You think that you're way faster."

He cocks his head to the side, like he's finding this whole exchange amusing. "I *am* way faster, Jaynie," he says smugly. "You simply can't win on your own."

"Pfft, we'll see about that," I scoff. And then I take off, leaving him in the dust. Or in the snow, as it is.

"Jaynie, Jaynie," I hear him call out.

I run faster, but it's not easy to gain traction in all the snow. It's far heavier in the park than out in the streets. My boots carry me as fast as they can, however, and I make a few elusive moves, ducking under branches heavy with snow, and to areas where the pines are thick and Flynn won't easily see me.

Still, I can hear him laughing not all that far way. I don't even know if he's searching for me at the moment. I think he's just feeling free, like me, seeing as we've never had carefree fun like this. Even when we snuck off at the Lowry place, there was always the fear of getting caught and facing retribution.

But not anymore.

I stop for a minute and just peer up at the night sky. Snowflakes land on my face, melting as they do. A few even hit my eyes, making me blink. I put out my tongue and find out what snow tastes like. "Nothing," I decide. "It tastes like nothing."

"Oh, Jaynie," Flynn sings out, with a tone that indicates he clearly believes he's won. "Looks like I've got you now."

"Hey, think fast," I yell as I lob a handful of snow at him.

I take off, and the race is on.

The snow is so deep where I've turned that soon I'm slipping and sliding down a pristine-white slope that looks like it leads down to the river. Ironically, it's the same river that brought me to Lawrence nearly six months ago.

Wow, this night is so different than that one.

Back then I was running for my life, whereas this night, I'm running for fun.

With a feeling of freedom that leaves me dizzy, I clamber down to the river. I sense Flynn is not far behind, but he's letting me enjoy this moment.

Soon enough, however, I hear him laughing.

He's definitely really closing in, so I juke left, then right.

And then I hear nothing.

"Hey, where'd you go?" I say as I spin around.

I see then that Flynn has fallen not too far away from where I've stopped. It looks like he may have slipped and crashed into a giant snow drift.

"Ha, serves you right," I call over to him as I place my hands on my hips.

I'm totally teasing, but when he starts to groan, his falling isn't so funny anymore.

I run over to him. "Crap, Flynn, are you really hurt?"

"Ow, ow, fuck yes," I am told.

Flynn bends his leg, bringing his knee to his chest. He grabs at it and says, "I think I hurt myself really bad here. I twisted something, for sure. And fuck…it hurts like a mother."

I drop to my knees and cover his hand with mine. "God, I am so sorry, Flynn. Do you think if I try to support your weight you can stand up?"

"I don't know," he says, grimacing. "Maybe."

"Just tell me what to do," I cry out, feeling helpless.

He smacks at the snow on the far side of his prone body and says, "Why don't you try putting one foot over here."

This is puzzling already, but a say, "All right."

Unsure how it is even remotely helpful, I place my booted foot where he indicated, leaving me hovering over his body. At that weird angle, I have no choice but to hold myself up so I don't fall on top of him.

"Now what should I do?" I ask.

"Keep that foot there, and lower yourself to your knee that's on this side of me."

I do as he asks.

And then I'm saying, "Um, this is really awkward." I frown down at him. "Tell me again how this is helping you get up?"

He ignores me and continues with more of his convoluted directions. "Okay, now place your hands up on either side of my head."

Once I comply with that directive, I'm straddling him.

And that's when he begins to laugh.

"What's so funny?" I say. "I thought you were hurt."

"Gotcha," he murmurs as he reaches up to caress my cold cheek.

"Flynn"—I smack his chest—"you're such an ass."

I'm not mad, not in the least. This is the kind of silly fun we never had in the past. And soon I am laughing right along with him. When I'm near hysterics, I fall to my back into the mushy snow.

Once I've recovered from my laughing attack, I roll to my side in time to catch Flynn making a snow angel.

As his legs and arms plow through the heavy snow, I prop myself up on an elbow and ask him what I already know, "What the hell are you doing, you foolish guy?"

"What's it look like I'm doing?" he volleys back.

Before I can answer, he says, "Just get over here and join me. We can make a snow angel couple."

I join him without hesitation, as I'm already reminded of one of our best memories from the past.

"This is like the day you made the pine-needle angel," I say, a reference to one of the first times we were ever alone together.

There was a place up in the woods on the Lowry property that we designated early on as all ours. A beautiful copse of tall pines encircled our secret spot, with soaring cliffs nearby. We dreamt of escape up there. And then I *did* escape when I jumped from one of the cliffs. But before that time came, that was where Flynn and I would go to shut out the world.

Someday I want to go back there with him, to our secret spot. Someday I know we'll need to go back, in order to move on.

But until that day, we have the here and now. And Flynn is saying, "This is better than the day I made the pine-needle angel."

I slow my movements to a stop. "Why do you think that?" I ask, curious.

He sits up. "This time we're not hiding. There's no need to run.

We have nothing to escape. This is just you and me doing what we want."

He's right. He's so damn right.

"It feels good, Flynn," I say as I stretch my arms way above me. "It feels really, really good. God, I want to stay out here and play with you all night."

Leaning toward me, and then slowly rolling on top of me, he whispers seductively, "So, let's stay and play."

Chapter Fifteen

Flynn

*U*nfortunately, it's too damn cold to stay in the park and play. Well, let's just say it's too chilly for what I have in mind.

Once I have Jaynie back in our room, however, all bets are off.

Wet, snow-covered clothes are peeled from our bodies and scattered across the hardwood floor. There's giggling and fumbling as we fall onto our bed.

Damn, Jaynie's damp skin pressed to my own cool flesh feels so fucking erotic. There's just something about being cold in some places...and really warm in others.

"Are you warm enough, baby?" I whisper as I press my cheek to hers.

"Mmm, I am, Flynn. I am." She writhes beneath me.

"Are you wet?" My voice is raw and husky when I ask her that. She groans, and I add, "You are, aren't you?"

"Yes," she hisses.

"Mmm..." I let my fingers roam, with a verbal promise of "Let's make you even wetter."

Minutes later, all I hear are her cries of, "There, Flynn, there… Yes, touch me like that."

Smug in the knowledge that I know Jaynie's body as well as my own, I bring her to where she needs to be in no time at all.

But I'm not done yet.

I then trail kisses down her body till I reach her heat. And then it's wet on wet—me licking, tasting, and just straight-up loving my girl.

Her hands find purchase in my hair, where she grabs hold and pulls at the strands. Hard, then harder, she tugs, her hips quivering under my hands as I give her what I have to offer—pleasure.

"Almost, Flynn," she chants. "I'm… almost… there."

And then she is there, quivering and quaking. I move up her body afterward till we're face-to-face.

One shift of my hips and we're joined.

But it's not enough.

I press my hips to her and push myself in as far as I can. "I want you, I love you, I need you," Jaynie pants in response.

I want and need her too. "I love you," I say as we move as one. It's smooth, so smooth, because we're good at this.

I am close, so close. So, when Jaynie pleads, "Harder. Go harder and faster, Flynn," I fall over the edge.

Afterward, I hold her in my arms, this beautiful girl, this love of my life.

The snow continues to pile up outside, leaving our little bedroom window painted in streaks of powdery white.

"I wish we could stay like this forever," she tells me as we both peer out the window. "I like being snowbound with you."

Leaning down, I kiss the top of her head. "I know what you mean. It feels like…" I search for the right words. "I don't know… I guess it kind of feels like we're the last two people on the planet."

"It does," Jaynie agrees, laughing lightly. "And I like that."

"Me too," I reply.

I decide then and there that this is another one of those moments I'll need to hold on to—this beautiful memory of how Jaynie and I played and loved on a late-season snowy night, a night where it was only us.

We had the world to ourselves that evening, if only for a few blissful hours.

The snow stops the next day, but our little world of Lawrence is still a wintry wonderland. The ground, blanketed in white, sparkles and glows under the sun of a new day. Like woodland creatures emerging from too-long hibernation, people venture out, bleary-eyed.

They're weary at first, but soon they come to life. By afternoon, the sandwich shop is flooded with customers. It's so busy that I have to grab an apron and help Jaynie.

"This is a first," I remark.

"It is," Jaynie agrees. She then hands me an order pad and pen. "Now get to work."

"Yes, ma'am."

Things eventually slow down, and when we finally have some time to ourselves, Jaynie says, "Wow, I think that was finally the last customer."

"We must've sold thousands today," I reply.

"That doesn't happen often. Bill will be happy."

"Yeah" I agree, "he will."

She then wants to know, "Did you make a lot in tips?"

I fish out a handful of bills and some coins from my apron pocket. Depositing the money on the counter, I say, "Between this, your tips, and the money I've been bringing in from my other job, we should be able to buy a car real soon."

"Damn." Jaynie shakes her head. "I can barely believe it."

"Believe it, babe."

"Flynn, this is great."

Smiling, she nudges me out of the way so she can reach the coffee pot on the shelf behind us. As she pours herself a well-deserved cup of java, and me one as well, she states, "Let's celebrate with some good strong coffee."

"Sounds good to me," I laugh.

As we hit the caffeine, Jaynie remarks, "It's been a long time since we've worked side by side like this."

"It has," I agree.

"It was fun... Whoa, hold up a minute. This coffee is way too strong. Can you hand me two of those." She gestures to a bowl of creamers.

I hand her what she wants, and then say, "Back to what we were talking about. I like working side by side with you. It's how we work best." With a wicked grin, I amend, "But then again, we also tend to work pretty well with you on top...or me over you—"

"Flynn!" She smacks my arm, but she can't hide her grin, or her blush.

Just as I'm about to pull her in for one hell of a hug, someone comes up behind us and clears their throat. Turning simultaneously, we find ourselves face-to-face with Detective Silver.

"Hey!" Jaynie exclaims, still cheery from our goofing around. "What brings you over to our little neck of the woods? Good news about the excavation, I hope."

Sighing, the detective takes a seat at the counter. "More like no news," he replies solemnly.

I watch as my girl's face falls. "Oh," she murmurs.

The detective asks for a cup of strong coffee, which we have plenty of. I pour him a huge serving, 'cause he sure looks like he could use the pick-me-up.

"You want cream or sugar?" I ask, holding the mug aloft.

"No. Black is fine," he tells me.

I set the coffee down in front of the him, then grab a stool out from the corner behind the counter. Once I've plopped my ass smack dab across from him, I rub my hands together. I have questions for this man, and lots of them. The first of which is, "How in the hell can there be no goddamn news on the case?"

I'm riled now, and Jaynie sidles up beside me to calm me down. Placing her hand on my arm, she says softly, "Flynn, please. I'm sure the detective is doing all he can."

Peering across the counter, she surprises the hell out of me when she puts him on the spot. "You *are* doing everything possible to solve this case, right?" she asks pointedly.

I resist the urge to laugh. Jaynie sure has come a long way. Watching her challenge the detective proves just how much progress she's made. We both have really made giant strides lately.

"Of course I'm doing everything I can to wrap up this case." Detective Silver clears his throat. "We all are. The state wants the Debbie Canfield case closed as soon as possible."

He takes a quick sip of coffee, all evasive-like, and Jaynie frowns. "Don't you mean the state wants the case solved? Not just closed, right?"

"No, I'm afraid 'closed' is what they're asking for now."

"That doesn't inspire confidence it will *ever* be resolved," Jaynie mumbles.

Tiring of all this double-talk, I set down my cup with a clatter and say, "Just lay it on the line, Detective. What are you trying to tell us?"

He takes a sip of coffee, then releases this long, drawn-out sigh. "I'm sorry to have to be the bearer of bad news, but the sad fact remains that we've excavated every inch of that old barn. And as of this afternoon, we've found absolutely nothing."

I raise a brow. "And that means…?"

"It means, Flynn, that if we don't find some evidence soon, this case is in real danger of being closed for good. Pretty soon I'll be forced to write up a report. I'll have no choice but to state that the girl, Debbie, must have run away, despite her last known whereabouts being at the Lowry house."

"Crap," Jaynie mumbles.

Taking another sip of coffee, and following a thoughtful pause, Detective Silver continues. "Perhaps this girl did indeed meet an untimely end. But without some kind of hard evidence, there's no way to build a case against Allison Lowry. Or anyone else, for that matter."

"Come on, though. We can't just give up." Jaynie's voice is verging on panicked. "I just know… I mean, I actually *feel* like it was Allison who hurt that girl."

Eyeing her intently, the detective says, "Remember what we talked about last time we were together. We can still build a case against Allison, for whatever it is she did to you. Assault and battery may not keep her behind bars forever, but it'd certainly tie things up and preclude her from an early release this summer."

Looking away sharply, Jaynie murmurs, "I still need time to think about it. I just don't know if I can do it."

The detective stands and places his hands on the counter. "Please, Miss Cumberland," he says, his tone pleading. "Give this some serious thought. I can take a statement from you at any time. You still have my card, right?"

Jaynie's lips are pressed together tightly. I can tell she's striving to stay composed.

"Yeah," I say, answering for her, "we have your card."

"Well, call me when you reach a decision. In the meantime, I'll keep you abreast of any new developments at the Lowry property.

But, let me say again, it does not look promising."

And with that downer, he walks out the door, taking all the peace and solace of the wintry weekend along with him.

Chapter Sixteen

Jaynie

"What do *you* want to do?" Flynn asks me after the detective leaves the sandwich shop.

I shrug, unsure of where to go from here. I know what I *should* do. But talking about what I went through is easier said than done. Plus, will it even matter?

Nonetheless, Flynn insists, "I think we should try and get back to Detective Silver as soon as possible. You have to decide whether or not you want to give him a statement and let him know either way." He stops and runs his hands through his hair. "I have to say, though, that it's not looking good up at the Lowry property. The old barn is apparently nothing but an old barn. Not a burial spot, after all."

I sigh. "Yeah, seems not. Still, Flynn, I don't know. I hate the idea of Allison being released early, but I really can't imagine how much help a statement from me will be in keeping her locked up."

"Detective Silver told you it could keep that bitch behind bars for quite some time. That should be more than enough motivation,

I'd think."

"It's not you who has to talk," I snap.

Shit, what am I doing? I'm not really mad at Flynn. He's only trying to help. I know he just wants me to reach a place where I feel comfortable telling my story—the *whole* story—to strangers.

But the truth remains that I'm scared as hell.

"I'm sorry I snapped at you," I say.

"It's okay, Jaynie."

He looks so dejected, and I know it's because of this one thing I keep bottled up. In any case, I at least owe him an explanation as to where I'm at.

"Look, Flynn." His eyes meet mine, and I try to smile so he knows I'm not mad at him. "Part of me wants to give a statement," I go on, "but I'm terrified it'll send me reeling backwards. You know, like back into a total funk?"

He nods. "That is always a possibility," he concedes.

I appreciate him not bullshitting me, and I add, "What if that does happen, and I can't get out of it this time? Flynn, seriously, things were so bad when you were away that some days it took all I had to get out of bed."

"But you did," he reminds me.

"Yeah, I kept going, but I wasn't, like, really *here*. I wasn't living, not at all. I only existed. I went through the motions of life, but with no heart in any of it."

"You *were* living, though," Flynn insists.

"Barely," I counter.

He takes a tentative step toward me, compassion clear in his sad, gray eyes. "I know it felt impossible back then, but that feeling never beat you." He scrubs a hand down his face. "Christ, it kills me that I wasn't here for you. I feel responsible. You should never have had to go through all that shit alone."

"It wasn't your fault," I say, shaking my head. "You *couldn't* be here."

"I know, but still… I'll never forgive myself for failing you."

"You didn't fail me, Flynn." I go to him and give him a hug. "God, we're so broken," I whisper.

"We're doing much better, though," he mumbles into my hair. "You especially are. I wish you could see yourself the way I see you."

Leaning back, I ask him, "Do you really believe that?"

"I do. You've made great progress lately, Jaynie."

Warming up to the idea that I may be able to do this statement thing, I say, "If I talk with the detective about what happened, you'd be with me every step of the way, right?"

He gives me a look. "Do you even have to ask that question, babe?"

"No," I admit. "I guess not."

He then assures me, "We'll get through this the way we work best, the way we always do things—together."

"You know what?" I touch the little scar below his eye.

"What?"

"I love you."

"I love you too, babe. And"—he catches my hand—"you got this."

"Then I think I've made a decision," I whisper.

"What have you decided?"

"I'm going to do it. I have no choice, not really. Not with the excavation going so poorly." I blow out a breath. "I'm going to call Detective Silver and tell him my story. And then we'll go on from there."

He tightens his arms around me. "You're doing the right thing," he says. "Though I'll always wish it was my statement they wanted instead of yours. I swear I'd take your place any day if I could."

"I know, Flynn," I tell him.

And I know he would too. So would Mandy. But their stories are not what the detective wants. My story has lifelong implications.

"I'll be there with you the whole time," he assures me again. "And if they need any corroboration, or whatever, to your story, I can help with that."

I hold on to my lifeline—this boy who loves me beyond bounds, this boy who makes me recognize my own strength.

"Thank you, Flynn," I whisper. "Thank you so much."

I mean it for so much more than just today.

*I*t takes until evening for me to build up enough courage to make the call to Detective Silver. And like Flynn promised, he is right there by my side.

In our room, with both of us perched on the edge of the bed, I hit "call."

When the detective picks up, I'm in no mood for small talk. I get straight to the point. "This is Jaynie Cumberland. I'm ready to make that statement."

After a pause, the detective replies, "Excellent. Can you hold on a minute?"

I don't know why there's a delay, but I say, "Uh, okay, sure."

Flynn, seated next to me, pats my knee encouragingly.

When I glance over at him, he gives me a 'you-got-this' smile, and mouths, "You're doing great."

"It's only been a minute," I say back, laughing.

Ah, now I see what Flynn is doing—distracting me, putting me at ease.

It works, until I hear the detective shuffling around papers and realize he's preparing to take notes. Damn, this is real now.

I mutter a cautious, "Here we go."

"Okay," Detective Silver says when he returns to the phone. "This is how it's going to play out. I'd like for us to meet up as soon as it's good for you—so I can take a formal statement—but until that time, me jotting down a few notes now will tell me how much evidence we have to make a case."

"All right," I murmur.

I remind myself that this is me taking control.

A few seconds later, Detective Silver, adopting a much more business-like tone, says, "As I understand it, you were physically hurt by Allison Lowry. Is this correct?"

"Yes."

At my trying-to-be-strong tone, Flynn reaches over and takes my hand.

"We'll go through the events leading up to the assault when we meet in person, but for now, I need to ask, were the injuries you sustained of a serious nature? In other words, was there significant harm done to you? Harm which required medical intervention?"

Was there significant harm done to me? And could I have benefited from some medical intervention? Yeah, that would've been nice. Maybe I wouldn't be facing a life of infertility if I'd been able to see a doctor.

Swallowing the lump that's threatening to close up my throat and shut me down, I croak out, "I miscarried because of Allison, Detective Silver. She kicked me in the abdomen, over and over again. She beat the hell out of me, really. So yes, I'd say there was significant harm done to me… And to my baby, who never even had a chance."

The detective pauses. And then he says in the kindest of tones, "Miss Cumberland, I had no idea. I am so sorry for your loss."

"Thank you."

Flynn squeezes my hand.

"Well, this takes Ms. Lowry's offense to a whole new level," he then informs me. "May I ask which hospital you went to, Miss Cumberland? With the records they have on file, we'll be able to throw the book at Alli—"

"Wait," I interrupt, panic rising. "There are no records. I never went to a hospital that night. I couldn't. For the love of God, I was running for my life!"

I start to sob, but even over my anguished cries, when the detective replies, I hear all too clearly that this admission, this fucking pouring out of my heart, has all been for nothing.

"I'm sorry, Miss Cumberland," he states. I hear his pen clink to whatever surface he's been writing on. "Without hospital records documenting your injuries, there's no way to prove Allison ever laid a hand on you."

I can no longer hold back. I am racked with sobs. It's like Allison still has the power to put me in my place. "She will always beat me," I mumble, defeated.

I drop the phone.

Allison is going to walk this summer, and there's not a damn thing I can do about it.

Chapter Seventeen

Flynn

"We must come to accept that which we cannot change. Take comfort, however, in knowing there is a bigger picture at play in the universe. Yes, we may be blind when it comes to what the Lord has in store for us, but trust me, my flock, He will never give us more than we can bear. And, eventually, we will see the light."

I'm listening intently to the minister, leaning forward on the pew, even. But not Jaynie. Nope. She's too busy fidgeting next to me. She hasn't heard a single word. Perhaps bringing her to church, to listen to this sermon, wasn't such a bright idea.

Confirming my suspicions, she leans in to me when I sit back and whispers in my ear, "Can we go soon?"

"In a few minutes, okay? Hang in there, the service is almost over."

Jaynie sighs, loudly. She's clearly not pleased with my response. Smoothing the light cottony material of her latest thrift store find, a lavender-colored dress, she lets out an irritated groan.

Despite her agitation and restlessness, my girl still looks so pretty today. All dressed up, and with her usually loose auburn hair pinned up in a messy bun, I can barely keep my eyes off her.

Too bad she's so unhappy with me. If she wasn't, the first thing I'd do when we get out of here would be go home, let her hair down slowly in a cascade of curls, and shimmy that sheath dress right the hell off of her.

I don't think that'll be happening, though. Not after I dragged her to this Sunday service.

Attending church was all my idea. When I first threw it out, Jaynie looked at me like I'd gone crazy. I guess because we're not overtly religious people. Still, I was hoping she'd find some solace in the minister's words, especially when I saw in a bulletin someone left in the sandwich shop and it indicated today's sermon was to be about 'accepting that in our lives which we cannot change.'

From the look on Jaynie's face at the moment, though, and her clear desire to go home, I think I was hoping for too much.

It's a shame too, since we have a problem—a big problem.

Ever since Detective Silver informed us that without hospital records there is no case to build against Allison, and with the excavation of the old barn still looking like a bust, Jaynie has fallen into a serious funk.

Not only have her nightmares increased in frequency, but she's been hoarding more food than ever. Plus, there's a new development. Jaynie has taken to fastidiously cleaning our little apartment every Sunday, like—no pun intended—religiously.

The significance isn't lost on me, Sunday used to be cleaning day at our former foster home.

"Oh, one more thing," Jaynie blurts out, a bit on the loud side.

The white-haired lady on the other side of her shoots her an admonishing glare, along with an annoyed, "Shhh!"

Jaynie sheepishly replies, "Sorry, ma'am."

In a greatly lowered voice, Jaynie cups her hand around her mouth and says to me, "We need to stop at the grocery store on the way home. I'm out of that Scrubbing Bubbles stuff. You know the one, the cleaner I like to use in the tub."

Oh, I know it. I know it all too well. We've never had such a sparkling clean tub, all porcelain-white and shiny as all get out. The sink is amazing too, and the toilet. Plus, don't even get me started on the glowing linoleum floor.

Despite the rigorous Sunday cleaning Jaynie has adhered to, she sometimes wakes up in the middle of the night simply to shine up something anew. I caught her just the other night when I got up to take a piss.

There she was, on her knees in the bathroom, scrubbing our already shiny-as-glass tub. As I whipped out my dick and let a stream of urine flow into the pristine toilet, she informed me—as nonchalantly as if we were having a discussion of the benefits of cleaning in the middle of the day, instead of in the middle of the night—that the tub absolutely had to match the sterile cleanliness of the sink.

"Whatever you say," I murmured groggily. "They both look good to me."

"Of course you'd say that," she snapped back, eyeing me over her shoulder as I flushed the commode. "You don't see all the dirt like I do, Flynn."

"I guess I don't," I conceded, knowing then for sure that this cleaning obsession was another symptom of the bigger problem.

I was then ordered to squirt some of that blue stuff in the toilet. "Let it soak," she told me. "You can go back to bed. I'll get to it after the tub."

She resumed scrubbing, and I left.

Heaven help us, but I truly think Jaynie believes she can scrub and disinfect our worries away. That's what this latest obsession is all about.

Ah, if only things were that simple.

But if this new cleaning craze helps her cope, who am I to make her stop? I fear the alternative, anyway.

Patting her knee, I say in a comforting tone, "Sure, babe. We can stop at the store."

Later, when we arrive back to our apartment—after the detour to the grocery store, of course—Jaynie shrugs out of her dress, and then throws on a pair of white boy shorts and a pink tank top.

Sighing, I sit down on the edge of the bed.

When Jaynie heads to the bathroom, as I knew she immediately would, she grabs up a sponge and the new can of cleaner we just bought.

"Do you want any help?" I ask as I unbutton my dress shirt.

She turns to me and purses her lips. "No, I think I got this," I am told.

"All right, Jaynie."

I shrug out of my shirt, and then, taking preemptive action, I open the window a crack to dispense with all the fumes that will soon fill the apartment. I then finish undressing. Once I'm down to just boxer briefs, I flop back on the bed. "Shit, I'm exhausted," I mumble.

I really am tired, though it's more mental exhaustion than physical toll. In any case, as I listen to Jaynie's rhythmic scrubbing in the other room, I am eventually lulled to sleep.

I'm awoken a short while later, however, when a warm body is flattened against mine, one I notice rather rapidly is devoid of all clothes.

Immediately stirred—in more ways than one—I open one eye and look up. "Jaynie," I breathe out.

Her hand closes over the hardening bulge in my boxers, making me gasp. "What are you doin', babe?"

She slips her hand down in my underwear, causing me to

instinctively lift my hips to grant her better access.

"What do you think I'm doing?" she rasps as she slides my boxers down my legs.

This is another new development—Jaynie wants sex all the time. And sure, we always desire each other, but this is different. She's disconnected. She just wants to give me head and fuck.

Like now, her head is already between my legs, and within seconds she's bobbing up and down on my cock.

Jesus. That feels good.

I should stop her, I know. But I can't. I'm a raring-to-go eighteen-year-old male, for fuck's sake. If she's looking for sex to take away her pain, I'm her guy.

After sucking me off just to the brink, she stops what she's doing and climbs up my body. "You ready for me, Flynn?" she asks, her voice all husky.

Hell, my response is to line her up with my cock.

As she lowers herself down on my length, she chants, "Oh-my-God, oh-my-God."

Seems Jaynie found God today, after all. Just not in the way I was hoping she would. This wasn't what I had in mind when I took her to church this morning, but, shit, I can't complain. Sex is a damn good escape for me too.

Flipping Jaynie over and onto her back, I drive into her in the way I know she likes it these days, hard and fast. Hell, who am I kidding? I like it this way too.

"Fuck," I mutter as I try and hold off on my release, mostly by thinking of things other than how hot and wild this abandoned sex is.

It's difficult to stay focused, though. Especially when Jaynie starts scraping her nails down my back and screaming out shit like, "Fuck me harder, Flynn. Oh, yes, that's so fucking good. I love your fucking cock."

That does it. I lose myself inside her, leaving me caught up in nothing but my release.

And for that little delicious slice of time on a Sunday afternoon, all worries are forgotten.

Chapter Eighteen

Jaynie

I'm floundering, I know it. And I can't deny that I really need to stop this craziness. The hoarding, the compulsive cleaning, the nightmares, and my insatiable need for sex—all these things are indicative of my mental state, which is currently fucked-up.

Short of seeking professional help, for which Flynn and I have no money, I can't come up with any good solution. His attempt to insert religion into my life was sweet, but I had to tell him church just isn't for me. Not at this time. I'm still angry at God for all I've lost.

Time is not my friend, either. Instead of healing old wounds, it seems the passage of the days, and then the weeks, only serve to cut open my psychological wounds more deeply than ever. Because no matter how you slice it, every day that goes by is a day closer to Allison Lowry being released from prison.

But then, just when I'm convinced all hope is lost and I am truly going off the deep end for good, a lifeline is thrown my way.

It happens on a warm evening at the very end of April, when

I'm working my shift at the sandwich shop. The smell of spring is hanging heavy in the air, having been ushered in throughout the day with a steady flow of customers.

But the day is almost over, and I'm rushing around to close out for the night.

When my work is finally complete, I lock the front door and prepare to head upstairs to Flynn, who arrived back from his own job a short while ago.

But then, just as I'm making my way up the stairs, my cell phone rings. I pull the device from my pocket, thinking it's probably more bad news of some kind. But when I see Mandy's name on the screen, I figure it's something positive. It is! To my delight—the first delight I've felt in a while—Mandy invites us to a birthday celebration on Saturday for the twins.

Knowing I'll be seeing my 'family' soon makes me feel better than I have in a while.

"Wild horses couldn't keep us away," I tell Mandy right before we disconnect.

Upstairs in our room, I relay the news of our invite to Flynn. To which, he replies, "Talk about perfect timing. We needed something like this to lift our spirits."

He really means me, but I agree and say, "Absolutely."

"Wow," he remarks as he flips back the covers on our bed. "The twins are going to be thrilled when they see all of us are there to celebrate their birthday."

Flynn is ready for bed already, clad in boxer briefs and a tee. I grab my own sleepwear and start putting it on. "I think the party will be good for everyone," I say quietly.

As he crawls into bed, he says, "It's great that we have our own car now too. We won't have to borrow Bill's. Plus, now we can stay as long as we like. Cody won't be disappointed that we have to leave at such-and-such time."

"Yeah," I agree.

One positive development as of late is that we recently reached our first savings goal and were able to purchase a car. It's just an old Ford Focus, one that looks like it rolled off the assembly line a long, long time ago. But, damn it, it's not terrible. And, better than that, it's all ours.

As I tug my sleep shorts up my legs, I add, "Having our own transportation sure makes planning a day like this much easier."

Flynn fluffs up the pillows so he can lean back against them. When he has them the way he likes, he says quietly, "It'll sure be nice to see Cody again. To tell you the truth, I can't wait."

It's touching how much Flynn loves Cody. I stop what I'm doing so I can smile over at him.

"It'll be nice for both of you," I say. "It seems like we've been working so much and dealing with all that case stuff all the time that we haven't seen Mandy and the twins in freaking forever."

Flynn folds his arms across his chest. "Well, now we'll see them real soon. And it's always a good thing when we're all reunited."

"It is," I agree. "It sure makes me feel better."

He pats the space next to him. "Come on, come to bed. Let's get some sleep. Work was a bitch today and I'm ready to crash."

"Okay, one sec."

After a quick pit stop to the bathroom, I crawl in bed next to a clearly very drowsy Flynn.

"Nothing bad happened at work today, right?" I inquire as I place my hand on his smooth chest.

"No, no, nothing at all," he replies, yawning. "It was just the usual—another long-ass day."

I kind of want sex, but Flynn is clearly beat. I watch as his eyes flutter open, like he's trying to stay awake. But after a minute, they close and he's dead to the world.

"Men," I murmur. "How can they fall asleep so damn easily?"

I'm tired, but sleep never comes easy for me. And tonight, after a good forty-five minutes of tossing and turning, I just give up. Slipping out from under the covers, I head to the bathroom to raid my candy bar stash.

There's comfort in routine, and after consuming a bar and a half, I feel pretty even-keeled. Chocolate, and the invitation from Mandy, has lifted my spirits, but I know I'm quite a long ways from well.

Still, I don't feel the need to compulsively clean anything on this night. And, later, when I finally do find sleep, I only have one minor nightmare.

And that, for me, signals that there's hope I will someday be whole.

Chapter Nineteen

Flynn

*S*aturday arrives, and by mid-morning, Jaynie and I are making the trip up to Morgantown for the twins' birthday.

When we arrive, I discover Josh is home this time. I finally get to meet him, and we hit it off just fine. We shoot the breeze while Mandy and Jaynie head to the kitchen to get things ready for the party.

But even with the girls out of the room, the twins are still running around, interrupting us every five seconds and making my interaction with Josh limited, at best. I'm actually glad when, a short while later, Mandy has a sudden crisis and sends us on an unexpected errand to pick up more ice cream at the convenience store down the road.

Finally!

It's my first opportunity to talk with Josh with no one around and no interruptions. A little man-to-man time never hurt anyone, and I've found it usually results in some unexpected disclosures.

To move things in that direction, when we leave the house and are walking across the lawn to his truck, I remark to Josh, "Wow, Mandy sure is a flustered mess today. It's usually not like her to go off the deep end over something as small as not having bought enough ice cream for the party."

"It's more than that," Josh mutters.

Ah, there is something I'm missing here. I suspected as much when Jaynie opened a tub of Neapolitan a short while ago, only to discover it'd been dug into pretty good. She mentioned this to Mandy, who then started wringing her hands. Mandy also turned about ten different shades of red. And then, after apologizing to everyone in the room, which seemed really unnecessary, she asked me and Josh to go buy more.

"What do you mean, it's more than that?" I ask once we're in the truck.

Buckling his seat belt, Josh says, "It's just that Mandy should have bought more in the first place. We could have avoided this whole situation."

Situation? Since when is ice cream a crisis?

When Josh nervously runs a hand through his blond hair, I sense he needs to talk. Hey, I know *that* feeling all too well.

"What's really going on?" I ask him.

He releases a pent-up breath. "It's just… Mandy, sometimes…"

"What?" I press.

"Okay, I'll tell you. But know in advance, this is gonna sound crazy."

"I doubt that," I murmur.

He blows out another breath, along with a nervous laugh. "Okay, so, here's the deal. Whenever there's any ice cream in that fucking house, I swear Mandy can't keep her hands off it."

Whoa, this sounds familiar. "Go on," I prompt.

"Well, take last night, for example. I caught Mandy in the kitchen, at, like, three in the morning. She was shoveling these huge spoonfuls of that Neapolitan stuff like it was the last thing she might ever eat. Dude, it was crazy." He shoots me a sidelong glance, to which I nod. "Anyway, I got her to stop. But she must've gone back downstairs once I was asleep so she could eat more."

Shit. So Mandy deals with issues similar to Jaynie.

It's somewhat surprising to me, since she always seems so together. It shouldn't be, though. We all deal with food issues, even the twins. Still, Mandy is always so strong and sure of herself, she was especially so when we lived in the same house. Not that there was ever any ice cream available to dig into.

Nor were there candy bars.

Sighing, I say, "Hey, you're not alone, dude." I feel like a new bond has been forged with Josh. "It's the same deal with Jaynie," I go on. "She keeps a stash of candy bars hidden in our bathroom. Has them all stuffed up under the sink."

He shoots me a sad, commiserating smile. "It's tough sometimes, isn't it? It's like you want to help them so fucking much, but you have no damn idea how to fix things."

"I don't know if it's possible to fix anything," I say. "Hell, I've called out Jaynie on the candy bars a time or two. But, really"—I lower my voice, ashamed—"I have no room to lecture her."

I don't elaborate any more than that. There's no reason to tell Josh that I have my own supply of candy bars stowed under a loose floorboard in our closet.

You know, just in case.

"Wow." Josh shakes his head. "I guess there is no fixing it, then."

"Dude…" Now it's my turn to run *my* fingers through *my* hair. "If you saw the conditions we once lived in, you'd totally get it."

"Yeah, well, from what Mandy *has* shared with me, it sounds like you guys had it rough at the Lowry house."

"You can't even imagine," I mutter.

When we return from the store with the ice cream, I overhear

Mandy whispering to Josh, "If there's any left, please just throw it away."

He nods. "Okay, hon."

A few minutes later, we push all that negative garbage behind us in order to make Cody and Callie's birthday a success. After all, it is their day.

After we regroup in the living room, Mandy sneaks off to the kitchen to grab the cake. A few seconds later, she's back, carefully balancing a sheet cake that's decorated with balloons made of colorful icing. Birthday candles, nine of them in all, glow brightly on top of the cake.

The twins jump up from the floor and clamber around Mandy. "Is that for me?" Callie asks, pointing to the cake.

Her eyes are wide as saucers, the flames from the flickering candles reflecting in her gaze. I realize then these kids have probably never had a birthday cake for their birthday. God, that hurts my heart.

"The cake is for you *and* your brother," Mandy tells her.

"Yeah," Cody interjects, side-eyeing his sister. "Cake for me too."

"Those two are hilarious with their bantering," Jaynie murmurs to me.

"They are," I agree, a smile brought to my lips.

Mandy slides the cake onto the coffee table, and Cody drops to the floor. He just sits and stares intently at all the colorful icing balloons.

"It so pretty," he whispers in awe.

Jaynie nudges my arm and murmurs, "Better than nutrition bars, yeah?"

"Much better," I agree, shaking my head as I recall last year and my sad attempt with Mandy to make the twins' birthday special.

Mandy starts humming the opening notes of "Happy Birthday," our cue to start singing, and I catch her eye. When she smiles over at me sadly, I know she's also remembering last year.

"You made up for it today," I mouth once we're done singing.

That makes Mandy smile.

Later, once the candles have long been blown out, and the kids have dug into their cake—like literally, as in we let them eat with their hands since it's their day—I pull Mandy aside.

"Hey, I just wanted to tell you again that you really made this day special for the twins." I nod down to Cody and Callie, who are sprawled out on the floor, smiling and laughing, still eating cake. "Those two are truly happy today."

Mandy closes her eyes. "God, Flynn, thank you for saying that. Their happiness means so much to me." She opens her eyes and peers up at me. "I swear I try, I really do. But I still find myself questioning if it'll ever really be enough."

"What do you mean?" I ask. "You're doing a great job with the kids. You always have."

"Thanks for saying that, but it's just… They've been through so much, you know?"

"We all have," I reply.

"Yeah, we sure have," she agrees, sighing.

"The twins are young," I remind her. "They're more resilient than us. Plus, because of *you* fostering them, it's really like they're out of the system."

"Yeah," she says, her tone laced with regret, "I sure wish I'd gotten out of the system at eight."

"I think we all wish that for ourselves, Mandy."

"We do what we can, though, right?"

"Yeah, we do."

My eyes meet hers and I realize for the first time that, despite her I've-got-it-together demeanor, Mandy is broken too. Hence the ice cream eating issues. I wonder what else she's dealing with in the aftermath of what we went through.

"I'm just glad I have Josh to keep me sane," she tells me. "He helps me keep my shit together."

Josh is over on the sofa, talking with Jaynie.

Jerking my chin in that direction, I say to Mandy, "He seems like a really good dude. Is he still getting along well with the twins?"

"Oh, good God, yes," she exclaims, her expression brightening. "Cody and Callie love him to death. He may as well be their biological father."

A little tinge of regret hits me that I couldn't be more for Cody and Callie. But Mandy and I were never a couple; we never saw each other like that. The kids deserve parents who are committed to one another, and I would never begrudge them that.

"Are you still planning to adopt the twins?" I ask.

Mandy nods. "Yes, definitely. We have more classes to attend first. Plus, Josh and I need to be married."

I nudge her arm. "Ooh, Mandy Sullivan, someone's old lady. Who would've thunk it?"

She bats me in the arm, with a warning to, "Shut the hell up, Flynn."

"Okay, okay."

I dodge a few more smacks, and when my beat-down has concluded, Mandy says, "So, speaking of relationships... How's everything with you and Jaynie?"

"Fantastic," I reply immediately. "As always."

She chuckles and peers down at the paper plate she still has in her hand. Tiny crumbs, what's left of her slice of cake, lie submerged in a puddle of melted ice cream. Not one to waste food—none of us ever would—Mandy raises the plate to her lips and slurps down what's left.

"Good to the last drop," she remarks as she deposits her empty plate in the trash bag Jaynie dragged in earlier for the spent plates and gift wrapping from the presents the twins tore into a short while ago.

"Always," I agree.

She dabs at her mouth with a napkin, and then says softly, "Can I ask you another question, Flynn?"

"Sure."

"Besides your relationship going well, how are you and Jaynie adjusting to the real world."

I shrug. "Eh, we're adjusting, I guess. To be honest, though"—I let out a sigh—"I think I'm doing better at it than Jaynie."

"Yeah?" Mandy leans back against the wall. "How so?"

"Well…" I glance over to the couch to make sure Jaynie's still wrapped up with talking to Josh. When it's clear she is, I tell Mandy, "Jaynie still has a lot of nightmares." She nods knowingly, lending further credence that her issues run deep too. "And," I go on, "this thing with Allison potentially getting out this summer has set Jaynie back in a lot of other ways."

Mandy doesn't ask for elaboration, not that I'd tell her. Some things are just way too personal.

Sensing my uneasiness at this turn in the discussion, Mandy narrows the topic to the investigation, which is far more welcome to me.

"Jaynie told me you met with the detective on the case," she begins.

"Yes, yes, we did."

Frowning, Mandy says, "She also told me about the excavation."

I shake my head. "Yeah, that. Nothing's come of it. At least, not yet."

After a long beat where I suspect she's thinking this through, Mandy says, "Why are the police so focused on just the old barn? Why not dig around in other places on the property?"

I blow out a breath. "Trust me, we wanted that to happen. But the detective claimed it wasn't realistic. Apparently, without a damn good reason, there's not a judge in this state who'll sign a court order to dig up the whole damn place."

"That's a shame."

"Yeah, it is."

We watch the twins play for a minute, and then Mandy says, "You know what, though, Flynn? All the property doesn't need to be excavated."

"What are you getting at?"

"Forget about the old barn, is what I'm saying." Mandy shakes her head. "What about the space where the *new* barn is located, the barn *we* worked in?"

She may be onto something. "Talk to me, Mandy," I say, urging her on.

"This is no sure thing," she prefaces. "All I'm going on here is pure speculation. It's just that ever since I talked with Jaynie, I've been thinking about the Debbie Canfield case. And I keep trying to pin where she fits into the timeline."

Intrigued that the always-clever Mandy might be on to something, I ask, "So, what'd you come up with?"

"Well, for starters, haven't you always wondered why a new work barn was built in the first place?"

I shrug. "No, I never really thought about it."

"Well, think about it now, Flynn. Think like Mrs. Lowry and Allison would have."

"Must I?" I deadpan.

"Yes," she replies. "Because from their perspective, you have to be thinking why spend that kind of money—money you could be lining your own pockets with, mind you—on a nice, new facility for kids you don't even care about. Why would they do that, Flynn, why?"

"I have no idea," I admit.

Mandy goes on, her excitement building, "Well, I think I do. Would they build a new work barn so we can have a better work environment?"

"Ha, right. No way."

"See, it just doesn't make any sense, not with those two. I mean, when did Mrs. Lowry, or Allison, ever care about doing nice things?"

"Never," I state.

"Exactly."

And then it starts to dawn on me. "Whoa, wait. So, just to make sure I'm clear on this, you're saying you think the new barn was built to—"

"—hide something in a place no one would ever suspect," Mandy finishes for me.

"Holy shit," I murmur.

Fuck, what if Mandy's right?

Chapter Twenty

Jaynie

"Well, that's it, Flynn. It's settled. We absolutely must go back to the Lowry property."

He groans, because he knows I'm right.

I crack the passenger window for some much-needed air as we pull away from Mandy's house.

"As much as I despise that place," I go on, "I just don't see how we can avoid a return visit. We need to check things out in the work barn, especially after hearing what Mandy had to say."

Flynn and Mandy shared what they'd been discussing—her new theories on the missing girl's body—shortly after the twins went to bed. I was immediately up for a return visit to the Lowry property. Flynn, not so much. I know it's only 'cause he loves me. But he worries far too much.

"I think we can avoid going back. If we want to, that is," Flynn says, his expression grim as I glance over at him.

His mouth is set and he's staring straight ahead at the road before us. His hands are clenched tightly to the steering wheel.

"And how do we do that?" I ask, curious as to what he has up his sleeve.

"We just call Detective Silver, Jaynie. We give him a heads-up on this new theory. He then takes what we give him and does all the investigating that needs to be done. Remember, the Debbie Canfield case is his responsibility. Not ours."

I let out a snort of disbelief. "I can't believe *I'm* the one having to talk *you* into going back to the Lowry property. Talk about an about-face on the subject."

"Why are you so dead set on going back there?" he asks, perplexed.

"Because we need more than Mandy's suspicions if we expect Detective Silver to schedule another excavation. Remember what he said about a judge issuing a court order for a more thorough search?"

"Yeah, he said we needed more evidence."

"Exactly! So let's go find some."

When we reach the interstate exit ramp for Lawrence, Flynn slows down considerably. I hadn't even noticed he was going so fast, but I guess he was. Stress can do that to you.

Exhaling, Flynn murmurs, "Jaynie, Jaynie…"

"What?"

"I think we need to talk about this."

"I thought we *were* talking," I counter.

"I mean a more in-depth discussion. There's a lot at stake here."

"Like what?" I genuinely want to know.

He glances over at me, one brow raised. "Well, for starters, your well-being is a huge concern."

Ah, Flynn is worried this will be too much for me, seeing as I'm already on shaky ground.

"Okay, pull over," I quietly state.

At the end of the ramp, there are several big, empty lots on either side of the road. These are turnouts where sleepy truckers can pull in and catch a few *z*'s. It's one of the larger ones that Flynn pulls into now.

I guess he's hoping no one bothers us. I don't see that as a problem. It's late and full night has fallen. The only things around are the crickets chirping in the background and the big full moon in the sky. Besides that, there's not a soul in sight, not even a passing car.

I stare out at the quiet darkness and say, "So, let's talk."

Flynn unbuckles his seat belt and twists to face me. His expression is already pained.

"Jaynie," he begins, "I know you're all gung-ho about going back to the Lowry house, but I suspect you're not fully thinking it through. Like, how about what going back there does to you? Returning to that place is like making a pit stop in Hell. Don't deny it. You know I'm right."

He is right, but this isn't about me.

Standing my ground, I say, "We *have* to go back, though."

"Not necessarily," he replies.

"What do you mean?"

"Detective Silver can just go talk with Mandy if he wants more input. Maybe he could even take her up to the property, have her look around the way we did."

"It *needs* to be us," I softly declare. "I feel like we started this journey with Detective Silver, and we need to finish it. Besides, Mandy lives too far away. And she has the twins to take care of."

He knows I'm right, but still he maintains, "I just don't know about this, Jaynie."

Flynn's real concern is clear, and I just go ahead and say what he can't…or won't.

"You're afraid I'll backtrack even more if things don't go well. You saw that I was making progress…until no evidence was found up in the old barn. And then it got worse when Detective Silver asked for my story and it was useless without hospital records to back up my claims."

"Jaynie—"

"No." I put up my hand. "Let me finish, Flynn. Let me talk it out."

"Okay," he whispers.

I take a breath, blow it out. This isn't easy, but it's time we lay it all out on the table.

"Now, you're scared," I say. "You're afraid if we go back and find nothing at all, I will end up worse than ever. And really," I scoff, "let's face the facts. I don't have that far to go to reach rock bottom."

"You were way better today," he counters, his voice so stressed, like saying it can make it true.

"Only because we were with Mandy and the twins. I'm sure I'll feel like shit by tomorrow."

"Jaynie, stop," he pleads.

But I go on. I have to. "You're worried I may eventually reach a point of no return, right?"

No response.

"You're right, Flynn. I could. But that might happen whether we go back or not. So see, we must go back. We have to try. If the outcome is good, it'll benefit not just the detective, but you and me."

"And if it's not?" he croaks out.

"I have to be honest. I don't know."

"Then, forget it," he hisses.

We need to address the elephant in the room. Or car, as it were.

Softly, I murmur, "You don't want to lose me, do you, Flynn?"

"No." He buries his face in his hands. "Fuck no."

I'm emotional, and so is he, but we need this all out on the table. "We're all we have in the end," I whisper, suppressing a sob. "And we know we can't lose each other."

"I'd die if I lost you," he chokes out. He hits the steering wheel with his fist. "Mentally, physically... In any goddamn way, Jaynie, losing you will kill me."

"But you need me whole," I whisper. "Me fucked up like I've been is no good."

"I just want you to feel happiness again. And it seems the longer this shit goes on, and the continued bad outcomes, the more elusive that becomes. I want you to know what it's like to not have nightmares all the time, to not feel hungry, even when you're full. I want you to want me because you love me, not because my dick in you makes you feel full."

"Flynn..."

"No, seriously, Jaynie. The way we've been living has to stop. Or at least, we need improvement."

Defensive and feeling prickly from hearing the truth, I say, "You have issues too, Flynn."

"I'm not saying I don't. But fuck me. All I care about is you. I love you. I want you to feel good again. I'd give anything, Jaynie, even my life, if it meant you'd heal."

"Stop it," I cry out. "Don't even think such a thing. I'd never heal if you were gone."

He yanks me to him, and I crawl over the center console so I can straddle him. It's not sex we're seeking, not today. We simply need to feel each other and be close. We are so tied together, and I realize then that his well-being is dependent on mine. I absolutely have to get my shit together. Not just for me, but for Flynn.

With my hands in his hair, I pull his head back so he has no choice but to look at me. This is me being strong, this is me fighting back. For me, but mostly for Flynn.

"I love that you have my back," I say. "God, I love that. And I love your fierceness in protecting me. But I promise, Flynn, from here on out I'm going to be strong. It's not going to happen immediately, and it's not going to happen in a straight line. But I'm willing to do everything possible to heal."

With his gray eyes watery, he says, "Promises are tricky things,

Jaynie. You haven't forgotten that, have you?"

"No. But I won't fail you. Not on this. However, it has to start with going back to the Lowry house, especially now that we have this new lead. I'm going at this head-on. And I need to you to do that, as well."

There's something else I want to do back on that property, something that can only happen up in our secret spot, up by the cliffs and in the ring of trees. For now, though, I keep that desire quiet.

At last relenting, Flynn finally agrees. "Okay, Jaynie, We'll go back."

I release a breath I didn't realize I was holding. "Let's give this all a purpose," I throw out, "something beyond healing. Let's make this about closure, for everyone. Let's find justice for Debbie, and get this case solved for the detective."

He chuckles. "You realize you're starting to sound like *you're* the detective on the Canfield case."

"I feel like it some days," I joke. But then, in a more serious tone, I add, "Maybe I should think about becoming some kind of an investigator someday."

Flynn smiles up at me—in support, not jest. "Maybe you really should."

Our futures are important, we both know that. Flynn makes decent money working construction, but I can't work the counter at the sandwich shop forever. It simply doesn't pay enough.

In that moment, I make another decision, one I hope may also help me cope. It's something that just may keep me sane through all of this, by giving meaning to this endeavor, no matter what the outcome.

I place my hands on Flynn's shoulders. "Hey, I was thinking—"

"That could be dangerous," he interjects.

He's joking around again, which is good. We need levity in this conversation. That's what we do sometimes when topics become too heavy.

Still, I smack his upper arm. "Hey, I'm trying to be serious here. I just had one of those… Wait, what do you call it when something you couldn't figure out before suddenly becomes clear?"

Flynn shrugs, his muscles flexing beneath my hands. "I'm not sure."

"Oh, wait, I know." I lift one hand and snap my fingers. "An epiphany, that's what I had."

"Okay. Go on…"

"I may have just now figured out a way to cope with everything before us—the missing girl case, dealing with the detective, going back to the Lowry property…yet again." My eyes meet Flynn's curious gaze as he tries to anticipate what I'm getting at. He needn't bother since I flat-out tell him, "I plan from this point forward to view this investigation like it *is* my own. I don't know about becoming a detective down the road—that might be a bit too much for me, criminals and all that—but I think I'd like a job that involves helping children. I could someday maybe help kids who are lost, like how we were…and how we still are, at times."

"I'm liking this idea, Jaynie," he says.

Encouraged, I add, "I'd like to go to college someday and earn a degree. Maybe then I could become, like, a special investigator for social services."

Flynn touches my cheek. "I think you can do anything you put your mind to, sweetheart."

The unwavering belief he has in me gives me more strength than I ever knew I even had.

"Dream big, babe," he adds.

"Yes, dream big."

I call on all my reserves and, with a newfound confidence I've not felt in a while, I declare, "It's settled, then. We'll go back to the Lowry property, and we'll keep going back, until the day comes when this case is solved. We're going to do this for Debbie Canfield and to right all the wrongs of the past. But, most importantly, we're going to do this for our own future."

Chapter Twenty-One

Flynn

We don't inform Detective Silver of our intentions. Before we take that step, we need to know if we have anything. And that means one more search on our own.

When Jaynie and I choose to return to the Lowry property, it's at the end of a warm day in May. The drive over is quiet and uneventful. We drive with the windows down, and the radio on, almost as if life is completely normal.

Until we arrive, that is.

Then it hits me, and I feel the need to make jokes. I don't know why. Maybe because I have an alternative plan if we don't find evidence, one that could end up putting me—and maybe Jaynie, but not if I can help it—in danger.

"Here we are," I sarcastically murmur as I'm rolling up the window and cutting the ignition. "Back again at our one-time prison."

Jaynie shoots me an admonishing look. "That's not funny, Flynn."

"Yeah, I guess it's too soon for bad one-liners."

She just rolls her eyes at me.

Even though we're parked in front of the gate, Jaynie and I stay as we are. We make no move to get out of the car. Attempts at bad jokes aside, I know we need a minute to fortify ourselves. Coming here is never fun. And this is actually very serious business. Jaynie's probably thinking the same as I am—thank God we got out of here alive. Debbie Canfield, the poor girl, never had that chance.

And that's why we need to do what we're about to do.

"Are you ready?" I ask.

"Uh-huh," Jaynie replies.

Still, we stay as we are.

I look around, not all that anxious to exit the car myself. The surrounding fencing is more ragged than ever, filled with more gaps, all unevenly cut and of varying sizes. All this new damage despite several recently erected 'No Trespassing' signs.

Releasing a pent-up breath, I again prompt Jaynie. "Now are you ready?"

"Yeah, I think."

I need her to move first, so I know she's okay.

"Well, good, let's get out of the car and get started. We're losing light." It's only early evening, but it's not summer. The days aren't all that long this time of year. "Babe?" I prompt when my commentary is met with silence.

Eyes glued to the driveway, or rather to the work barn and the house that are visible up in the distance—the leaves on the trees are mere buds still—she mumbles something indecipherable.

Hand going to her knee, I ask, "Hey, you sure you're up for this?"

Despite Jaynie's numerous declarations of how this is something she *must* do in order to move forward, I have my doubts. Her nightmares have been worse than ever, and the compulsive cleaning and hoarding candy bars have reached epic levels. Just the other day, I opened the cabinet beneath the sink and sixty chocolate bars—yeah,

I counted—tumbled out, right onto the spotless linoleum. Spotless I say because, damn, that floor has been gleaming.

I turn the key in the ignition, the resulting click loud as a gunshot in the silence. "I'm starting the car. We can come back another time. This is clearly a bad idea."

Jaynie grabs my forearm, keeping me from turning the key the additional click that'll bring our rattle-trap car to life.

"No, Flynn," she says, softly but firmly. "We're doing this."

"Are you sure?"

"Yes." She sighs. "But there is something I want us to do before we start searching the barn."

"What's that?" I ask, clueless as to what this new development could be.

Hedging, she says, "Let me start by saying this is something I think we *need* to do, before we do anything else. I've thought about this for a long while, even before we ever agreed to come back. And definitely the other day, out in that empty lot."

"Okay…"

"It's something I can't do alone. And I wouldn't want to. *You* need to be there with me for this to work."

I still have no idea what she has in mind, but I tell Jaynie what I will always tell her. "Anything. I'll do anything you need me to do."

She slides her hand down my forearm and grasps my hand. "Follow me, then."

We step out of the car and, with Jaynie in the lead, crawl single file through a large gaping hole in the fence.

Then, with our hands clasped in solidarity, we start up the driveway.

We pass the house, the excavating equipment long gone. The search of the old barn is clearly over.

We continue on till the work barn fades into the distance. We trudge through the fields, the grass beneath our sneakered feet dewy from the heavy evening air.

We hike all the way up to the old barn, where all this time I assumed, for no particular reason, that this is where we'd stop. But no. Right past the old structure we cruise.

Finally, when we reach the tree line, and then step onto a familiar trail in the woods, a trail we've traveled many, many times, I have an idea of where we're heading. Jaynie is leading me to our secret place. We're going to the one location on this property that we can stomach. It's a place that has healed us many times before.

"Ah, now I understand," I murmur.

She smiles over at me. "I knew you would."

With the reflective silence this journey now seems to require, we walk through the forest side by side. The foliage is sparse, but the trees themselves are huge and looming, the underbrush, a tangled and thick web of brown that requires us to step over or go around every few feet.

Nothing stops us, though. We know the way.

At last, we reach the edge of a soaring cliff. It's the same cliff Jaynie jumped from on that fateful and final night.

She lets out a shaky breath and squeezes my hand. "This is it, Flynn. This is where we parted."

Suddenly choked up with emotion, memories race at me as fast and furious as the dark water rushing below. I raggedly confess, "I didn't know if I'd ever see you again after that night."

Jaynie turns to face me. She takes my other hand in hers. "I wasn't sure I'd survive that jump, either. The water was so cold."

She shudders and I lift her hands to rest on my shoulders, my own hands finding purchase at her tiny waist.

"You did it, though, sweetheart," I say in a hushed tone. "You survived it all, Jaynie. The jump, the water, the journey to Lawrence… And now we have our life together, just like we always planned."

She peers up at me, shaking her head. When she finally speaks, her voice is nothing short of pained. "I wasn't supposed to be so broken, Flynn. I never dreamed I'd end up so fully and utterly fucked-up."

Tears form in her eyes, turning the depths a placid green. I lose myself there for a minute, until I have to force myself back to the present.

"You're not fucked-up," I adamantly declare. "And you're not broken. You're a girl who's been through a lot. And you're healing. You are. It doesn't happen overnight, you know?"

"I know," she says. "But I haven't been doing much healing lately, have I? It seems for every step I take forward, I take three or more steps back. The wounds just keep ripping open wider and wider, no matter how much fixing we try to do. And what if we turn up nothing in the barn? Where does that leave me, Flynn?"

Not finding anything worthwhile in the barn is a real possibility, but I'm sick of leaving our future in fate's hands.

"How do we stop that from happening?" I ask, desperate for answers, desperate to help this girl I love. "Your pain is mine, Jaynie," I say, feeling myself break further. "I feel when you're hurting. I feel when you're sad. I feel you right now, in fact, and I know you're fucking dying inside, despite everything we talked about that night"

"I'm trying," she sobs. "I'm trying so hard, for you. It just isn't working as fast as I'd like."

"So how can I help?" I ask. "I want to do something. I'll do anything I can to make your pain stop."

Grasping at my shoulders, her fingers digging into my flannel shirt, she hitches the material up.

Tilting her head back, she closes her eyes, and whispers, "Make it stop, Flynn. You have the power. In this place, you could always make me forget anything and everything. That's why I wanted to come up here before we do anything else. That's why you had to be with me. I need you to do what you always did to make the pain stop. Make me stronger so I can endure whatever happens, good or bad."

I know exactly what Jaynie wants, what she craves. Near the end of our time in this godforsaken place, when life started to turn really bad, we'd sneak up to this secret spot to be alone. And once we were by ourselves, we found solace in becoming one. We felt like we were dead inside, but coming here and making love made us feel alive.

She whispers, "Please, Flynn, give me back my life."

I lean down and touch my lips to hers, soft nipping kisses and then, more urgently. I nudge her mouth open, allowing our tongues to touch. Those deep kisses make me hard in no time, and I hoist Jaynie up so she can wrap her legs around me.

With my hands in her hair and our lips locked, I back her toward the copse of pines where we've shared all of our secrets and every inch of our bodies so many times before.

When I lay her back on a thick bed of soft pine needles, we finally break apart. Both of us are panting, and Jaynie is frantically pushing her leggings down over her feet. She digs her heels in the ground and slips off her sneakers, and then I toss everything off to the side.

Bare from the waist down, Jaynie spreads her legs and shows herself to me. "Flynn, look how much I want you."

I groan, because God, does she ever. All wet and pink and... "Shit. I'm right there with you, baby."

I shimmy out of my jeans and boxers, my rock-hard want for her springing free. Slowly, I lower my body to hers and with one shift, I'm home.

"Jaynie... God, Jaynie."

I want to go slowly, but I can't. She can't either. Urgency and the need to find healing to reaffirm this life we share overtake us.

For each frenzied thrust I give her, she rises to meet me. Her hands ply at my ass, urging me to go faster. I do, and soon her cries of pleasure are echoing off the tall pines as they watch us engage in a dance as old as time.

This is what Jaynie wants, and this is what she needs. She whispers those exact words to me, over and over. Maybe I need this too, this act of love that feels like we're confronting everything that's been holding us back from moving on.

This is so much more than what it appears.

This is the two of us going back to where we were.

This is us pulling ourselves out of the past, a past that was at once dangerous and full of death.

And this is us grasping at a future, one that is safe and full of life.

Chapter Twenty-Two

Jaynie

I'm on a high when Flynn and I leave the forest. I don't even care that we spent too much time in our secret spot and now the light of the day is dying. I needed that closure and healing, the kind only Flynn could ever give me, and only in our place. I needed it before we move on to the real reason why we've come to the Lowry property.

Despite what's ahead of us—searching for evidence of a young girl's demise—I feel better than when we first arrived. Now, I have the fortitude to do what we must. And even if this newfound feeling lasts for only a few hours, I know in my heart that healing is finally within my grasp.

We won't always need to come to the forest to find peace. Flynn is the key, and I can be with him here, or anywhere, and find that love. It was always here, and within me; I just needed to awaken it.

Hand in hand, Flynn and I emerge from the woods and make our way down through the fields. I can't help but glance over at my ruffled-hair boy and smile. His hair is mussed because of our time in the forest. It reminds me of old times, and better yet, the happier times ahead.

"You look like you're feeling better," Flynn remarks, one brow raised when he catches me staring.

"Hmm, I wonder why that is?" I squeeze his hand and add, "Seriously, though, Flynn. I know now that I'm going to be all right."

"I've always *known* you'd be fine," he replies. "I've always believed in your strength."

"Thanks, Flynn."

I feel so good, confident even, but some of that positivity dissipates when we reach the barn where we used to toil away the days. Memories of starving and being forced to work for hours on end slow me to a skidding stop in front of the big, sliding wooden doors, which now stand ajar and askew.

Despite my hesitation, I know I can do this.

Sighing, I nod to the wreckage in the dark, cavernous recesses of the barn. "I guess vandals got to this place too."

"Yeah," Flynn replies. "Remember how I told you that after my first trip back here."

"Yeah, I remember now." I nod, recalling how Flynn also shared with me how he kicked the shit out of one of the old work tables, simply to relieve all the stress coming back had brought him.

"I kind of feel like kicking something myself right now," I say under my breath, too low, by choice, for Flynn to hear.

"Hey, you know what…?" He lets go of my hand and turns to me. "Maybe we should come back another day. I think it's too dark now to see much of anything, and I sure as hell don't want you to trip over something and get hurt." Softly, he adds, "I think this place has caused you more than enough pain."

"There's no need to be concerned about my mental health," I counter, giving voice to what he's really trying to convey.

"It is something to consider, Jaynie."

He has my best interests at heart, but I decided when we were up in our secret spot, and when we were out in that lot off the ramp, that I'm no longer going to run and hide.

"You told me the other day that I was strong," I remind him.

"You are."

"So?"

"Yeah, okay, but why push it?" He grabs my hand once more. "Come on. Let's just get out of this place."

Not angry, but needing to stand my ground and let Flynn know I'm done with being a prisoner of fear, I twist from his hold. "No, Flynn. We have to do this, okay? *I* have to do this. And I can. I finally can."

He searches my eyes, and seeing the truth, he finally relents. "Okay, Jaynie."

He then slides one of the heavy doors open the whole way, only to reveal more darkness and the stench of spilled booze from all the partying that's occurred up here since this place was shut down.

Wrinkling my nose, I mutter, "Yuck. Let's just get in there and see what we can find as fast as we can."

In the end, though, Flynn turns out to be correct. Not about thinking we should've left in order to protect my emotions. No, I hold up just fine in the barn. It's something simpler—the lack of lighting in the building—that makes searching nearly impossible.

But, first, we do try.

Among the eerie shadows of turned-over tables and busted-up chairs, we look here and there. Even so, we find not a single shred of evidence to indicate a girl was ever buried in the barn.

The only thing of interest I do come upon, like a sad blast from the past, is the going-away card the twins made for Mandy last summer. They never had the opportunity to give it to her, however, since Allison kicked Mandy out of the house in the middle of the night, days before her planned departure that would've fallen on her eighteenth birthday.

"Check this out." I hand the folded piece of ivory parchment over to Flynn. "Remember when I found this card last fall?"

He nods, turning the paper over in his hands. "Yeah, I remember."

"Well, I meant to save it for Mandy back then." I sigh. "I guess that day I found it, I wasn't thinking straight. I must've set it down and forgotten about it. Shit, Flynn, I was so out of it by then I don't even recall doing that."

"There was a lot going on at the time," he reminds me.

I shiver, and it's not from the cool evening air. "There sure was," I quietly agree.

I glance away, and he clears his throat. After a beat, he unfolds the card, revealing Cody and Callie's pastel-inked heartfelt messages to the girl they've viewed as their mom long before they ended up in Morgantown with her.

We love you.

See you soon.

We promise to be on our best behavior so we can come live with you.

Don't forget us, Mandy. You're our mommy now.

Even in the near-darkness of the barn, I don't miss the tears that form in Flynn's eyes.

"I'm so glad the twins are with Mandy," I murmur.

"Yeah," he rasps, "I am too."

I wrap my arms around him as I reach over and glide my finger over the twins' sweet words. "We should take this with us and give it to Mandy, like I originally planned."

"We definitely should," Flynn says, before folding up and pocketing the card.

Before we depart we conduct one final search of the premises.

Coming up empty-handed the second go-round, Flynn insists we leave. "We'll come back another day," he says. But it's uttered with little conviction.

I nod and agree, but the truth is, despite feeling better than I have in a long while, we need a break from this place. Healing may have been found up in the forest, but we need time for it to set in, like fresh oils on a painting.

As we depart, our return looms imminent.

But it will not come tomorrow... or the next day... or the day after that.

Chapter Twenty-Three

Flynn

Jaynie is healing, finally. And it's a real kind of healing, not a back-and-forth dance between the past and the present.

I find out quickly that with healing comes change. Good, positive change and more than just one. There are changes for both of us, in fact.

One early morning, following a night with not a single nightmare, she and I come to a decision.

"I think we should ditch our secret stashes of food," I declare. "We should start living like normal people. What do you think?"

"Yes," Jaynie says, putting up no resistance. "I've actually been thinking that same exact thing."

This is good, really good.

We don't toss the food; that would be a waste. What we do decide to do is leave all the candy bars out in the open, on prominent display on the nightstand.

Fuck, that's still rough.

The next morning, as we're leaving for work, Jaynie remarks, "Shit, this feels weird. Leaving all our candy bars out in the open like that."

"We have to stay strong," I remind her.

"Yeah, I know."

When I still sense hesitation, I add, "It's not like someone's going to come in our room and steal them." I sound far more confident than I feel as I hurry Jaynie out through the door and lock up behind us. "We and Bill have the only keys," I go on. "And Bill would never let himself in to our apartment, not as long as we still live here."

"I know," she replies. "But it still feels strange, Flynn."

"I know, babe. But we'll get used to normal soon enough."

Hours later when we return from our jobs, the candy bars are still on the nightstand.

"See, I told you they'd still be here," I say, taking a seat on the edge of the bed.

Truth is this is a relief for me too.

Jaynie plops down next to me. "Well..." She reaches over and grabs two of them. "We may as well eat a couple."

She hands me one of the chocolate bars, and once we have them unwrapped I tap mine to hers. "Cheers," I say.

Laughing, she asks, "And just what are we toasting to?"

"How about..." I think it over, and come up with, "Let's toast to healing?"

"I'll agree to that any day."

So we toast and we eat chocolate. And afterward, we make love.

And the healing continues....

Jaynie draws up a cleaning schedule, one that is reasonable and includes me helping out. I'm all too happy to agree with sharing the cleaning duties. "After all, it's only fair," I say. "I live here too."

"Yes, you do, mister," Jaynie retorts, clearly teasing. "About time you start carrying your weight around this joint."

I give her a mock-salute. "Yes, ma'am, you are correct. I have been remiss in my duties to keep our apartment in tiptop shape."

We bust out laughing, but I know what's real. Jaynie is only adding me to the cleaning schedule to keep her on course.

No matter. Whatever works for her is cool with me.

The new schedule works out great. Well, mostly. The only times Jaynie has an urge to compulsively clean is after she's had a nightmare. Luckily, her bad dreams have lessened considerably. We deal with only one a week, sometimes two.

And that, my friends, is much better than one every night.

Chapter Twenty-Four

Jaynie

I'm feeling good. Really good. My life feels like it's been returned to me. But sometimes it's weird to make my own decisions. I spent so much time under the care and authority of others that it feels odd not to have to ask all the time, "Is this okay?"

One thing I do want input on, however, Flynn's input specifically, is a decision I must make at the end of May.

"Hey, I need to ask you something," I say to Flynn one weekend morning when we're lounging around in bed.

He leans over and kisses my forehead. "What's up, babe?"

I sit up. "I received a call from the women's clinic the other day."

"Okay...and...?"

"It was a reminder call that it's time for me to go in and get another birth control shot."

I look down and away, but Flynn tilts up my chin so he can see my face. "What do *you* want to do?" he asks.

I sink down into the pillows and turn to him. He lies down as well, putting us face-to-face.

"I don't know if I should bother," I say. "I mean, the doctor was pretty adamant that I will never be able to have kids. So really, what's the point of staying on birth control?"

"None that I see," he says quietly, his voice resigned.

God, I still feel so bad that I'll never be able to give this great guy kids. And damn it, Flynn would be so good with our children. How he is when he's with Cody and Callie shows me as much. He deserves to have children of his own someday, and I can't help but feel guilty, knowing I will fail him on that.

"Flynn…" I close my eyes, unable to look at him. "I'm so sorry," I choke out.

"Hey, hey, stop." He gathers me in his arms. "It's all right. Everything is fine." Stroking my back, he reassures me that I am all he will ever need or want. "In this lifetime, or in any other," he adds.

That leads me to my decision, finally. "I don't want to get another shot." I lean back so I can see Flynn's face. "I may never get pregnant, but I don't want to actively avoid it. Are you okay with that, though?"

He nods. "Yes, of course."

And so it is decided.

With all this healing, I begin to feel more outgoing. I start to think about one thing I've wanted to do for a long time. I just never felt up to it, until now.

I want to meet Crick, Flynn's friend. He's a part of Flynn's life, and I should get to know him. I inform Flynn of my desire, and together we make a plan to meet up with Crick the very next evening at a diner halfway between Lawrence and Forsaken.

On the way to the place, I confess, "I'm so nervous." My knees bob up and down. "I hope Crick likes me."

"Are you kidding?" He chuckles. "Crick is going to love you."

"You better be right." I sigh. "I just want to make a good impression for you. I don't want to come off like some scared little rabbit."

Flynn laughs. "Babe, I'm sure Crick is just as nervous to meet you. Remember"—he glances over and holds my gaze—"we're all broken here."

That we are. And that's what turns out to break the ice.

A short while later finds the three of us in a booth at the diner, laughing and talking, our dinner plates cleared. Flynn was right; I had nothing to worry about. Crick was way more nervous than I was about meeting. So much so that when we were initially seated, Crick ordered a Coke and proceeded to knock it over not ten seconds after it arrived.

"Shit, man," he said as syrupy soda flowed everywhere.

His eyes flittered from Flynn to me as he nervously pulled napkins from the dispenser on the table.

"Sorry, miss," he directed to me, his pale skin turning about twenty shades of red. "Please excuse my clumsiness. Oh, and my cursing."

"Don't worry about it. You're fine," I assured him. I then grabbed napkins on my own and helped clean up the mess on my and Flynn's side of the table.

Our waitress came over with a rag shortly thereafter and cleaned the table more thoroughly. She then brought Crick a new drink, and when she left he plucked up an ice cube from his lap and plopped it into his new soda, proclaiming, "Guess my clumsiness at least spilled the ice for us, yeah?"

Flynn busted out laughing. "Dude, you mean 'broke the ice,' not 'spilled the ice.'"

The three of us couldn't help but chuckle over the spilled-ice incident that did indeed 'break the ice.'

Our conversation moved on from there, and as of the last few minutes we're discussing our plans for the future. A topic that used to make me sad, but now makes me smile. Just knowing I *have* a future fills me with joy.

Noticing my grin, Flynn places his hand over mine. "Yeah, we got it all planned out," he tells Crick.

"Do ya now?" Crick replies.

"Yep," Flynn says. And then he proceeds to tell him, "Jaynie's going to be making an appointment over at the community college in Lawrence. She's ready to sit down with a career counselor and sign up for some classes. She has a dream, you know?"

Flynn is so proud of me. I hope I can live up to his expectations. *One day at a time*, I remind myself.

Crick smoothes back his stringy blond hair and asks me, "What's your dream, Miss Jaynie?"

"I'm hoping to someday help kids who are in situations like the one Flynn and I were in."

I've put more thought into what I want to do down the road, and I keep returning to the helping kids/social work idea. Flynn is fully onboard, of course. He's my biggest cheerleader, in fact. He even completed all the financial aid forms for me online, using Bill's computer.

Crick nods approvingly. "That sounds real nice. Giving back and all, that's what life is all about."

"For sure," Flynn agrees.

Crick picks up a straw and taps it against the edge of the table like it's a cigarette he's flicking ashes from. He must be jonesing for an after-dinner smoke.

Flynn, watching Crick flick the straw, says to him, "Hey, man, if you need to go outside and grab a smoke, we're fine with that. I'd join you, but I've finally quit for good."

"Good for you," Crick says, his tone revealing he's genuinely pleased for Flynn. "I'm actually trying to quit for good myself." He holds up the straw. "Been collecting these everywhere I go. I read somewhere that after you've weaned yourself from the nicotine, it's mostly missing the action of smoking that gets ya started again."

"Hmm," Flynn says, "that kind of makes sense."

We stay and talk for a while longer, but eventually we must go our separate ways. Not before making plans to meet up again sometime soon, though.

In the car, as we start heading home, I scoot over and lean my head against Flynn's shoulder. "Tired, babe?" he asks.

"A little," I reply. "Mostly, though, I feel relaxed. We had such a good time. I really like Crick. He's a good guy."

"He is," Flynn agrees. And then, with a smile creeping into his voice, he says, "And as for relaxed, relaxed is good. No. You know what?"

"What?"

"Relaxed is more than good. It's great."

"It is," I agree, yawning.

On the way home that night, I think about how our lives are changing, all in positive ways. The only thing hanging over our heads is the Allison Lowry situation.

But that's a worry best saved for another day.

Chapter Twenty-Five

Flynn

We put it off and we put it off...

And then one evening, right before bed, Detective Silver calls with the news that *it's* happening. That which we've allowed ourselves to forget as we focused on learning to enjoy our lives is about to occur—Allison is slated to be released from prison in July.

When I hit 'end' on the devastating call, Jaynie is just coming out of our bathroom. I inform her of the bad news immediately.

She pales and mutters, "That's only a month away, Flynn."

"I know." I take a seat on the edge of our bed and place my head in my hands.

"We have to do something," she says.

"Like what?" I mutter, out of options.

Jaynie throws her hands up in the air. "I don't know, Flynn." She sounds exasperated. "I guess we better do what we *should* have done before. We need to return to Forsaken and search the hell out of that property. There has to be something we missed."

"Like what?"

"I don't know, but there must be something."

"You're right, you're right." I run my hands down my jeans and stand. I always think better on my feet. As I begin pacing our small room, I give voice to my burgeoning thoughts. "We never properly searched the new barn, we know that. It was too dark the night we were up there to really see anything. You remember that night, right?"

My eyes meet Jaynie's and she blushes ever so slightly. She's so cute. "I remember everything about that night, Flynn," she whispers.

"As do I," I reply. I go to her and urge her to sit with me on the bed.

Neither of us will ever forget the time we spent in the forest, the way we re-connected. And hell, whatever we did that night worked, as both of us are doing better than ever. But we won't be faring all that well if Allison is released from prison. That bitch will surely seek out vengeance on Jaynie. Her hatred for my girl runs deep. I always wondered why that was, but knowing what we now know, it all makes sense. Jaynie resembles Debbie, the missing girl Allison most likely offed.

"I like our new life, Flynn," Jaynie says as she leans her head against my shoulder. "I don't want it to be ripped apart. Everything always seems to get taken from us."

She starts to cry and I hold her in my arms. "Not this time," I say, determined. "Nothing is going to change. I swear to you, sweetheart, I will not allow us to fall back apart."

"But we already are," she sobs. "Or at least I am. I haven't cried in weeks, and"—she lifts her head from my chest so I can see her puffy and tear-streaked face—"look at me now. This is me backsliding, Flynn."

"You're not backsliding, Jaynie. I won't let you."

And that is when I promise her that I will do everything in my power to make sure Allison remains locked up. No matter what it takes. Hell, I'll plant the damn evidence if it comes to it. And Jaynie doesn't know this, but I have the means to do exactly that. That's been my back-up plan for a while now.

Still, I hope it doesn't come to what would definitely be the commission of a crime, since the only thing worse than Allison's early release from prison would be for *me* to end up behind bars. I'd be unable to protect Jaynie, not to mention I'd be breaking every promise I've ever made to her.

Fuck, man, it just can't come to that.

Chapter Twenty-Six

Jaynie

The next day, we decide to return to the Lowry property.

It's a lazy kind of Saturday, but not for Flynn and me. We spend the entirety of the afternoon combing through the work barn and the surrounding outdoor areas.

When we find nothing useful, we search the house.

We even search the old barn again on the off chance we missed something when we were up here with Detective Silver.

It's an easy sweep of the old barn, since the excavation crew left the interior essentially destroyed. We find the stall walls torn down, the wood piled neatly in the corner, and the trunks emptied. And though the dirt floor has remained mostly intact, it's clear from the way our sneakers sink into the soil that several feet of the barn floor was dug up and sifted for clues.

Resigned that Allison must have covered her tracks so well that nothing will ever come to light to implicate her in Debbie's disappearance, I sit smack-dab in the middle of the mushy dirt floor and pull my knees up to my chin. I'd like to curl up in a ball and disappear, but the best I can do right now is lower my head to between my knees and close my eyes.

Blowing out a breath wrought with abandoned hope, I quietly declare, "We're screwed, Flynn."

I feel his warmth as he sits down beside me. "Hey," he says encouragingly, "we're not out of options yet."

I lift my head, open my eyes, and gape over at him. "Are you high? There's clearly nothing up here to implicate Allison of anything. I'd say that equates to us being screwed."

He frowns. "Just because we haven't found anything doesn't mean there's nothing here."

I'm at the point of near exasperation. Can't he see the truth?

"Jesus, Flynn, there's no evidence, okay? It's time for us to accept it."

He reaches around to the back pocket of his jeans, and says quietly, "Maybe there is some evidence, Jaynie."

I watch, wide-eyed, as he pulls out a vial of blood. "Holy shit, Flynn! Is that what I think it is?"

"Yes," he replies, turning the vial over in his hands and peering at it like it may hold the key to everything. "It's blood."

"Who the hell does it belong to?" I ask, even though I have a feeling I know the answer.

Flynn says softly, "Uh, it just may be a sample of Debbie Canfield's blood."

"*May be* or *is*, Flynn?"

His eyes focus on me as he says, "It's Debbie's blood."

Like a thunderbolt, it dawns on me where this blood must have come from.

"Oh, God, Flynn," I exclaim, shaking my head. "You stole one of the vials of the missing girl's blood from Detective Silver? When did this happen? Did you take it during the car ride up the day we met with him? God, you must have. What in the hell were you thinking? And where have you kept it all this time."

"I kept it in a little cooler in the closet where I was keeping my candy stash," he says. "And as for what I was thinking, I was thinking it may eventually come to this."

"What does that mean?" I tentatively ask.

"Jaynie, I think you know."

I do, but I just don't want to say it. Flynn is going to use this blood to plant evidence.

"Flynn—" I begin.

He cuts me off. "I told you before that I'll do *anything* to keep you safe."

"Even if it means planting evidence," I whisper.

"Even if, Jaynie."

"Shit." I stare at the vial of blood. "How'd you steal it, anyway? I didn't notice anything amiss that day in the car."

I glance up at him and, and, proudly, he says, "I guess all that time as a runaway, me living as a kid who had to steal to survive… Well, I guess it finally paid off. Remember the heavy coat I left in the detective's car that day?"

"Yeah, I do."

Of course, I remember. Flynn was too hot, having not planned for an early spring warming.

He goes on. "Then you also probably remember how Detective Silver laid my coat on the front seat before we got out of the car."

"Yes, I do."

"He did that to cover the files and the blood. He even told us it was good I didn't need the coat, that I was actually doing him a favor since he could use it to cover Debbie's file and blood samples from prying eyes."

"Jesus, Flynn."

"Anyway, when we got back in the car, and I grabbed up my coat,

I also managed to snatch one of the vials of blood."

"But Flynn, Detective Silver had to have noticed a vial went missing. Funny he never mentioned it."

I'm at a loss as to how I should feel. Should I be elated or terrified?

"I guess he never noticed." Flynn shrugs, and we both stare at the blood. "Or maybe he thought he lost it. After all, there was a lot of opening and closing of car doors that day. One of the vials could've easily fallen out onto the ground."

"But a vial didn't fall out."

"No, it didn't."

"So what happens now?" I ask.

Flynn tilts up my chin so I have no choice but to tear my gaze from this blood that may turn out to be our saving grace.

With his steely gray eyes as determined as I've ever seen, he says, "Let's go find a knife."

Chapter Twenty-Seven

Flynn

I can't believe we're doing this. Or, rather, I can't believe *I* am doing this. But it's okay; I'll deal with the fallout if it ever comes. Jaynie doesn't need to go down with me. No need to have her directly involved with planting evidence.

Sure, she'll probably get in some kind of trouble if we're ever caught, simply for being at the Lowry premises while I did the deed. But if she doesn't actively participate, she'll be looking at nothing more than a slap on the wrist. Not too bad compared to what will happen to me.

"Flynn." Jaynie sighs. Her frustration with me not allowing her to handle the knife or the blood we're about to plant is showing as we get underway with our crime…or rather, *my* crime. "At least let me hold the knife while you pour the blood on it," she practically begs.

No way.

We're standing in the middle of the kitchen in the Lowry house. Or, more accurately put, we're in what remains of the kitchen. This room, like all the others in the house, has been ransacked. The table and chairs that once sat in the middle are busted to small pieces. Their scattered remains lie about, along with cabinet doors that have been ripped from the hinges. All the drawers have been pulled out as well, their contents strewn all over.

This cluttered mess made finding a good, sharp knife easy enough. There was one particularly lethal-looking blade wedged behind a broken chair leg. I picked it up and wiped it off, hopefully leaving it devoid of fingerprints.

But now I've reached the hard part—making this kitchen knife look like a murder weapon.

"I'm good," I insist as Jaynie once again asks if I need assistance.

As I hold the handle of the knife with one hand that I've wrapped in an old dishrag, a measure taken to prevent transfer of my own prints, I balance the vial of blood in my other hand.

"I'm just going to pour a little bit of Debbie's blood here and there," I murmur.

"That should work," Jaynie says, nodding encouragingly.

I tip the vial to pour the blood, but then I re-think my strategy.

"Hey, maybe I should pour a lot, and then wipe the blade off. That's probably what someone would do with a bloody knife they're planning to hide, right?"

Jaynie sighs. "I don't know, Flynn. Just hurry, okay?"

Her eyes flitter about, like someone might walk in on us at any moment. I'm pretty certain that's not going to happen, but there's no telling her that. Now that we're in the commission of a pretty major crime, she's a nervous wreck, convinced that the police are going to do some random property check and catch us red-handed.

"I think I'll pour and wipe," I decide, at last.

"Whatever. That'll work."

I kick out the edges of an old towel I placed on the floor earlier to catch any dripping blood. "We should probably plant this towel with the knife," I muse, more to myself than to Jaynie. "It'll look like Allison used it too, seeing as it's hers."

Jaynie found the old towel up in Allison's bedroom, kicked under what remained of her bed. I recognized it right away as belonging to Allison. The bubblegum pink color, her signature shade, gave it away.

Beyond the nauseating hue, however, I remember all too well from the days when Allison would prance around in front of me wearing only this towel, or one like it. Once she called me in to the adjoined bathroom and asked me to hand her what could've been this exact one. She was standing in the shower buck-naked, propositioning me with her eyes.

Allison was always hitting on me when I lived here, but to no avail. I despised that skanky bitch from the start. I couldn't even bring myself to hate-fuck her. Though I sure am fucking her now, and my actions are brimming with hate.

Yes, it's pure hatred I feel as I pour Debbie Canfield's blood all over the knife, the excess dripping to the towel beneath in big crimson globs. When I pick up the pink towel and start to wipe the excess blood from the knife—as I imagine Allison would've done with the real items, if they exist—I murmur, "I know you killed her, you bitch. This may not be real evidence, but it's going to be just as good."

With the deed completed, Jaynie and I head out to the new barn, the one we used to work in, to plant the knife and the towel.

The plan is to hide these two items in a hidey-hole I once dug in the ground. It's the only spot in the barn where one of the concrete slabs covering the floor ever came loose, which was kind of odd in a new structure. No matter. I noticed it last year and utilized the space beneath the slab as a hiding spot for food.

Five minutes later, I'm lifting up one end of that loose cement slab.

A centipede takes off as I quietly say to Jaynie, "The hole I dug is still here."

"It was always a good hiding spot," she replies.

"It was."

I carefully place the knife in a hole that's about two feet deep.

I then toss in the bloodied towel and quickly replace the concrete slab.

Standing, I turn to Jaynie and say, "Let's get the hell out of here."

Chapter Twenty-Eight

Jaynie

I have so many mixed feelings regarding what Flynn and I did in the barn at the Lowry house. Planting evidence would surely land us in jail, if we are ever caught.

Hopefully, though, our plan will go off without a hitch.

"When should we call Detective Silver?" I ask as soon as we return to Lawrence. "I'm just ready for this thing to end."

We're trudging up the stairs to our rented room, but the hour is late.

Flynn stops on the step above me. He turns to me in the darkness, his face cast in the long shadows of the stairwell. Even in the dark, it's clear he's also struggling with what we did.

Closing his eyes, he leans back against the wall in the narrow corridor. "I don't know, Jaynie… Soon, I guess."

He seems exhausted, though I suspect it's the effect of the mental toll that comes from what we had to do to stay safe from Allison. I wish I could bear more of his burden. I hate that he wouldn't allow me to be more directly involved with the planting of the knife and towel. Somehow, though, I have a feeling that by accompanying him every step of the way, even if I didn't handle the evidence directly, I'd still go to prison.

I think Flynn's coming to grips with that fact right now. And that's another reason why he's hurting.

I reach out and close my hand around his forearm. Well, I do this as best as I can. His arms are strong these days and corded with muscles.

"Hey," I begin, squeezing in what I hope is a comforting way. "We did the right thing."

Opening his eyes, he peers down at me. "Did we, though?"

"Yes, Flynn," I say insistently. "You know it was the only thing we *could* do. We were backed into a corner."

"Yes, we were."

"So what's really bothering you?"

He lets out a little snort, like a laugh, but not. "Maybe the prospect of watching you get carted off to prison has me a little down, yeah?"

I start caressing his arm. "Hey, come on. What's done is done. Should we go back to Forsaken and dig up the knife? Do you want to go throw it away? If we do that, you know what happens next. Allison walks free."

"No way is that happening," he says, suddenly adamant and ferocious.

There's my guy.

"Yes, exactly, Flynn." I nod and nod. "That's exactly why what happened *had* to happen. We did what we had to do." I'm more fervent than ever as I add, "I believe in what we did. We had no other option. Nothing was ever uncovered in the excavation and the case is about to be closed, right?" He nods, and I finish with, "This is justice for Debbie, Flynn. And protection for me and you."

Suddenly pulling me up to him, he holds on to me so tightly that

I soon can no longer discern if it's my heartbeat or his that pumping so strongly between us.

"Shh, shh, everything will be okay," I murmur. "Everything's going to be fine."

Whether I'm uttering that statement for Flynn's benefit, or for my own, I don't know.

But just like our indistinguishable heartbeats, it doesn't matter. What Flynn does for himself he also does for me. And what I do for me will always ultimately be for him.

We work this way, we live this way, we love this way—together, always, as one.

Chapter Twenty-Nine

Flynn

Jaynie is still set on calling Detective Silver basically as soon as we step in our room. But I want to wait.

"Just until tomorrow," I clarify.

"Why? Now is as good a time as any."

"Look…" I blow out a breath. "It's late. If we call him now, it looks really suspicious."

Hands resting on her hips, she questions, "And just how does it look suspicious? I thought we were going with the story that we happened to be in Forsaken today and decided to stop up at the property to look around for evidence one final time. He knows we don't want this case closed."

I turn away, mumbling, "He's going to be pissed we didn't inform him first."

Jaynie comes over to stand in front of me, so I have no choice but to deal with her insistence that we call Silver now.

"Listen," she says. "We're telling him it was a spur-of-the-moment decision, right?"

I nod. "Yes."

"Okay, so we explain that that's why we had no time to call him."
She pauses, like she's thinking it over. Then she adds, "Better yet, you
know how the cell service is up there, right?"

"Yeah, shitty," I reply.

"*Very* shitty. So it's believable when we say we *wanted* to call, but
there was no service. We have those crappy pay-as-you-go phones as
it is. It's a good story, Flynn."

I take a seat on our bed and run my fingers through my hair.
Why *am* I so hell-bent on putting off this call to the detective?

Do I have a good reason?

You bet your ass I do.

As soon as we make the call, there'll be no turning back. And if
Detective Silver figures out that *we* planted the phony evidence, we
are fucked.

Jaynie included.

Hell, I should have made her stay back here in Lawrence. I
should've done this on my own.

"We're waiting till tomorrow," I state firmly.

When Jaynie sees there's no changing my mind, she releases a
long sigh, effectively giving up. "Fine, Flynn. We'll do it your way."

Chapter Thirty

Jaynie

We make the call to Detective Silver the next day, just like Flynn wants.

Seated cross-legged on the floor of our room, facing one another, the morning light slants in through the window, illuminating the side of Flynn's head and making his sandy hair appear golden. He's stunning to me. Even the little crescent-shaped scar beneath his right eye, that gift from his asshole father, doesn't detract from his hotness factor.

He smiles over at me. "Here goes nothing," he says.

"Or everything," I reply, my own smile dying on my lips as the seriousness of what we're about to do sinks in.

Blowing out a breath, Flynn hits the speaker on the phone and dials the detective's number.

Thirty seconds later, he's sharing the story we devised.

Flynn lays out what we came up with—that we stopped by the property on a whim, to check one final time for evidence. He adds that we tried to call the detective, but didn't have any service.

"We were in the work barn," Flynn continues, his voice a little strained, but only detectable by me since I know him so well. "Cell service is never any good on the property, especially in the barn. Anyway, while we were there, I remembered an old hiding place where I used to stash food."

I can hear the detective loud and clear on speaker when he clears his throat, already not pleased with our taking things into our own hands. "Where is this hiding place, exactly?" he asks gruffly.

"On the floor," Flynn says. "Or, more like, *in* the floor, in the ground itself. It's a place I dug out, under a big concrete slab that came loose."

He goes on, explaining to the detective how he lifted the loose slab yesterday and started to dig, far deeper than where he used to hide food. "And that's when I uncovered what looked like a bloody towel," he finishes.

"A bloody towel, huh?" The detective sounds wary, if you ask me.

But Flynn forges on. "Yes, a bloody towel. And when I looked at it more closely, I could make out the outline of what looked like it could be a knife underneath. I didn't want to dig any deeper, though, and taint potential evidence. I just filled in the hole, and then Jaynie and I left the premises."

The detective is mad as hell, at first. He lets us know it too. "That was trespassing, what you two did. Do you realize that?"

"Yes, we know," we utter simultaneously.

"You aren't supposed to go searching around up on that property, not alone, and not now or ever. I told you to call me if you thought of anything else."

We apologize, again and again, and finally the detective calms down. He even goes so far as to grudgingly admit that it actually may be a good thing we found something to further the case.

"The Debbie Canfield files are about to be closed for good," he informs us. "I estimate they'll be asking me to wrap things up by the end of this week. It would've been sooner, but these things always seem to get bogged down in red tape."

"The case won't be closed now that there's potential new evidence, right?" Flynn asks. "They can't do that after what we found."

"Perhaps not," the detective responds. "But I must tell you that a bloody towel doesn't mean much, nor does a knife. At least, not without a DNA match to back those things up."

My gaze meets Flynn, and I nod.

He then asks the detective, "You'll send this stuff to a lab for testing, right?" His eyes never leave mine.

"Yes," Silver confirms. "Whatever we find will be analyzed for evidence."

Flynn and I let out a collective sigh of relief, knowing that the blood will be a match to Debbie Canfield.

I muster up the courage to ask a question of my own. "Detective Silver, when do you think you'll go to the property to check out what we found?"

He hesitates, like he's pondering, and, at last, he says, "Well, today is Sunday and most everyone is off. I'd prefer to take a full forensics team up with me since you mentioned possible blood." I hear the detective flipping through pages of what I assume is his planner. "Tomorrow I'm testifying on another case," he murmurs. "That'll take up most of the day." More page-flipping and then, "Tuesday looks good."

"Tuesday," I echo.

"Is it too much to ask for you to keep us updated?" Flynn wants to know.

"I always do," the detective reminds us.

"Yeah, yeah, you do," Flynn says, his voice a little guilty-sounding. "And, uh, thanks for that."

"No problem."

The call comes to an end.

"What do we do now?" I ask Flynn.

"We wait."

I'm off from work on Monday. Flynn takes the bus and leaves the car with me. I need the car for a good reason, one he and I have discussed at length…and one I feel is high time I get a move on.

I finally made an appointment with a career counselor over at the local community college, and she has me scheduled in for ten this morning.

At the meeting, things go better than expected. I end up leaving the school filled with hope that my dream of someday helping kids in a meaningful way may truly become a reality. Armed with course schedules for the fall semester, I climb into the car. After I deposit my packet of info on the passenger seat, I send a quick text to Flynn.

Hey, just got out of my meeting at the school. It went really well! The career counselor told me if I take my core courses here at the community college, everything should transfer to a four-year school, no problem. That'd be perfect, since even with aid we'll still have loans. This way, we'll save a lot.

Flynn texts back: *Babe, I am so happy for you. I knew you could do it. And I believe in you for the steps ahead of you too. You're going to be a star student, and someday you'll become to the kids you help what you already are to me—a saving grace.*

You're sweet, I text back. *I love you so much.*

I love you too, Jaynie-bird.

Smiling, I set the phone on the passenger seat and start the car. I'm all set to return to our rented room, but as I start driving my joyful feeling wanes. I'm bothered by a troubling thought, a thought that started as a nagging concern, but is now a full-blown worry.

"Hell with going home," I mutter as I make a turn to the road that leads out of Lawrence and toward Forsaken.

"You better hurry," I prod myself when I'm halfway to my destination.

I'm tapping the steering wheel like Flynn does when he's uneasy. Damn, I need to haul ass to the Lowry property if I'm going to be successful in saving the man I love.

See, I have to do something before I can even think of saving kids like me and Flynn. I need to save us, first. And that means I cannot allow Flynn to sacrifice his future to save mine. Not now that the future we dreamed of is within our grasp.

"We can't fuck this up," I whisper, hitting the gas.

I drive toward the work barn on the Lowry property, while there's still time to fix the mess we made. I need to get rid of that planted evidence as soon as possible. And that means I must get to it before the detective does, which is supposed to be tomorrow.

If Allison ends up released in a month, then so be it. The cost to keep her in prison is just too high. If we're caught, Flynn will be put away, just like his father. Damn, he could even end up in the same prison as his dad. And that would surely kill him.

I hit the gas.

Chapter Thirty-One

Flynn

I'm so happy for Jaynie, going after her dreams like this. There was a time when she could barely deal with people. She was that broken by the system. But finally she's strong enough that she actually feels she can help the kids society casts aside.

I'm interrupted from my reverie when the foreman yells at me. "Get a move on, O'Neill. You're on the clock. Daydream on your own damn time."

"Yes, sir," I reply.

He then sends me over to work in another area of the apartments we're building.

Fine, I can use the walk over to think about my own future.

I've been thinking about what I want to do, career-wise, a lot lately anyway. Working construction is all fine and good while I'm young and strong, but what will happen when I get older? I could always hope for a promotion to foreman, which would involve more overseeing. But even if that comes to pass, there's still the weather to factor in. Here in this part of the country construction is not really a year-round gig. At least, not a steady one. In the summer, like now, work is plentiful. But come winter, it's a whole new ballgame.

Sure, there are projects here and there, but it's not always something one can depend on. And that's not going to cut it. I need consistent, reliable employment if I'm serious about building a future with Jaynie.

And I am. More than anything else in my life, I want to do that.

But what sort of employment would I best be suited for?

When I think back to my time at the Lowry house, I have to admit that for all the bad times there were a few good ones. Meeting Jaynie is certainly at the top of that list, as well as forging what I know will always be lifelong relationships with Mandy and the twins.

The twins… I think about the time I spent with them, specifically their home-schooling. We older kids were responsible for teaching Cody and Callie all their school subjects, and we did a good job. I, however, was especially adept at helping Cody. He has difficulties learning in traditional ways, but that never mattered to me. I was always coming up with creative methods to teach him what he needed to learn.

Like this one time with math. Cody couldn't figure out how to count. I enlisted Jaynie and together we used craft materials—different colored wooden dowels, to be specific—to help Cody learn to add.

Maybe I could take some college classes myself, just like Jaynie plans to do.

Maybe I could become a teacher.

Hell, I think I'd really like that.

With a newfound purpose in my step, I stride to the new work area, only to discover all the other workers have stopped for lunch.

Sighing, I take a seat on a huge cement block, away from the other guys. I open my brown bag and pull out the creation I made this morning before I left the sandwich shop. But just as I'm about to bite into tasty roast beef and cheddar on five-grain bread, my masterpiece, my cell buzzes.

It has to be Jaynie, so I place my sandwich on the crinkled bag and answer the phone, all without checking to see who the caller actually is.

"Hey, babe," I say without pause.

"Um…" *Shit, not Jaynie.* "It's Detective Silver," the voice on the other end informs me. "This is Flynn O'Neill, yes?"

"Yes. It's me." I clear my throat, my cheeks warming at my silly misstep. "Sorry. I thought you were someone else."

"Clearly."

There's humor in the detective's voice, and I can't help but chuckle myself. But then, as always, he gets down to business.

"I called today to give you a head's up on the Canfield case, just like I promised I would."

"Hey, I appreciate that," I say. "So, what's up?"

"My court date for today was postponed," Detective Silver informs me. "So, it looks like I may have some extra time on my hands. I was thinking of driving up to the Lowry property to check out your lead on that potential new evidence."

"Whoa, that's great." I blow out a breath, both nervous and excited. I want the detective to find the planted evidence, sure, but I can't help but worry a little that he'll realize it's manufactured. "So you're heading up there, like, right now?" I croak out.

"Yes," he replies. "Though this is too last-minute for me to get a forensics team together. Still, I can take some photos and cordon off the area. I'll get another patrolman posted up there to stay the night. I had one on duty last night, but he's off today."

My voice cracks as I ask, "You had a patrolman on duty up there?"

"Absolutely. We wouldn't want to take a chance on vandals getting to the evidence you told me about before the authorities do, right?"

"Yeah, yeah, you're right," I murmur.

Shit. This is it. There's no turning back. I should call Jaynie to let her know the ball is rolling.

Quickly, I end the call with the detective, and then I try to reach Jaynie.

Unfortunately, there's no answer, which I find a little odd. Jaynie always picks up when it's me...unless she has no service.

But where could she be that she has no cell service?

Chapter Thirty-Two

Jaynie

*O*kay, so traipsing around on the Lowry property all by my lonesome is kind of terrifying.

Who knows what kind of weirdos could be lurking up here in the middle of a lonely summer day?

The silence is positively deafening as I walk more briskly up the long driveway. Seems even the birds have nothing to sing about today up in this hellhole. And then, as if things weren't creepy enough already, the wind starts to blow, making it sound as if the leaves on the trees are whispering to me: *Watch Out!*

"Crap," I murmur. "Stop with the overactive imagination already."

Still, I pick up the pace. Consequently, I'm down at the work barn in no time. Despite wearing cotton shorts and a thin tee, I am drenched in sweat.

Fanning myself with one hand and pushing the barn door open with the other, I mutter, "God, just make this fast, you fool."

It's unsettlingly dim in the work barn, and, of course, that's when

I realize I left my cell in the car. Not that it matters, since there's such spotty service up here. If I find myself in a bind, I'll be shit out of luck.

Pushing damp hair from my face, I hurry into the shadowy recesses and rush over to the area where Flynn and I hid the 'evidence.' Once I'm in the right place, I drop to my knees and get to work on removing the cement slab from our fake evidence hiding place.

Only problem I run into is that it takes a lot more effort than Flynn had to expend for little 'ole me to lift the damn slab off the ground. My clammy hands don't help matters. Seems it's nearly impossible to keep a firm grip on the edge of the cement, leaving it to slip and slide this way and that, but not in the direction I want it to go.

Finally, after a few tries, I have enough of a steady hold to heave the slab off to the side.

"Ugh." I fall back on my ass and suck in a few much-needed breaths.

After a couple of minutes spent recuperating, I'm back my knees and digging the loose earth with my hands.

Down, down, down I burrow, down to where Flynn buried the bloody towel.

"There it is," I blurt out when I spy the soiled item.

Grabbing the edge gingerly, I use it to lift out the knife we also planted.

As I rise to my feet, our fake evidence in hand, I stare down at the empty hole. For a minute I consider filling it in, but then I decide to leave it as it is. This way, maybe it'll look like a vandal or partier got to the knife and towel, leaving Detective Silver to conclude the same when he's here tomorrow.

I release a sigh as I think about the repercussions of making this move. Removing our manufactured evidence means Allison will receive her early release. Even though it's less than ideal, it's still a more palatable outcome than Flynn going to prison for planting evidence.

This was all a crazy, reckless idea from the start.

Resigned that this is the way it has to be—we have too much to lose otherwise—I head toward the big barn door that I left partially open. But I falter when a shadow suddenly appears across the opening, dimming the sunlit view.

"What the hell," I gasp.

Oh my God, what if there was someone in the house? What if it's some derelict with plans to hurt me?

I was hurt before by a sick man, and it took Flynn and his infinite amount of patience to help me heal.

Looking for a way out, I pivot left and right.

But there's nowhere to run.

Should I cower and hide?

No.

To hell with not fighting back. I will never again be a victim.

Scanning the barn, I search for something with which to bash in this potential assailant's head.

But then I realize there's no need to search for a weapon.

I already have one—the sharp knife with Debbie Canfield's blood on it is in my hand.

Chapter Thirty-Three

Flynn

I continue to call Jaynie. And she continues to not pick up.

"Damn it! Fuck, fuck, fuck." I kick at a stack of wooden planks that I'm supposed to be carrying, stubbing my toe in my fit of anger. "Ow, shit."

"Get moving, O'Neill," the supervisor on this side of the work zone yells over to me when he sees me stalling. "You can make calls and get pissed off on your own time, you hear me?"

"Yes, sir." I put my cell away and return to hauling material, though I continue to have a very bad feeling.

As the hours pass, my worry reaches epic levels. Quitting time can't arrive soon enough. But as things always go when you're in a hurry, the final hour of my shift passes more slowly than all the rest.

Finally it's five and time to go.

Since the bus runs late most days, I decide not to take a chance. Whipping out my cell, I call Crick and ask for a ride back to Lawrence.

"No problem, kid," he tells me after I inform him I'm in a hurry

175

to get home. "I was just finishing up with my own work day."

Five minutes later, Crick picks me up in his work vehicle and we head over to Lawrence.

"I thought you bought yourself a car?" he inquires a few minutes into our ride.

"Yeah, I did." I smooth back sweaty hair from my forehead. "But I left it for Jaynie today."

"Oh, yeah? Why's that?"

Crick's not generally nosy, he's just making conversation.

I then tell him, "She had an appointment this morning over at the community college. Remember how we were telling you she plans to take some classes this fall."

"Oh, yeah, that's right. She wants to help kids, right?" Crick smiles over at me. "I still think that's a really good thing."

"Yeah, yeah, it is," I agree.

I'm trying to sound upbeat and in the conversation, but the truth is I'm distracted and worried. I can't stop running my hands through my hair, pulling at the in-need-of-a-trim ends with every pass.

Crick, glancing over at my fidgety ass, asks, "What has you so worked up, man? Something other than schooling plans going on with your Jaynie?"

"Yeah, there kind of is something." I admit. "There may be a problem."

"Talk to me, Flynn."

Crick is a good friend, and hell, I need to talk to someone. Otherwise, my head might explode.

"It sounds stupid," I begin, sighing, "but I can't get a hold of Jaynie. It's not like her to not pick up. And last I heard from her was when she sent me a text, and that was way back around lunchtime."

Crick, viewing the situation more sensibly than I can, says, "That doesn't seem all that long ago. Maybe she got herself busy with some little project or whatnot. You know how women are. Always busy,

busy, busy with something."

He's trying hard to be reassuring, but I know that's not it.

"Nah, Jaynie's not really like that," I reply.

When we reach Lawrence, I give him directions to the sandwich shop. But when I see our car isn't parked out in front of the store, I ask Crick to drive around to the back.

"There's an alley in back where we sometimes park," I inform him.

"No problem," he says.

As soon as he hangs a right into the alley, though, I'm mumbling, "Aw, shit. The car's not back here either."

"I'm sure she's okay," Crick says.

But I'm insistent. "Nah, man, I got a bad, bad feeling."

Chapter Thirty-Four

Jaynie

*W*hen my would-be assailant walks into the barn, I am ready. Hovering just inside the doorway, I grasp the handle of the knife Flynn and I planted. It's still wrapped in the bloody towel as I raise the blade high above my head, ready to slash.

And I am willing to do more. Whatever I must do in order to survive, I will.

The stranger enters the barn, and I close my eyes.

Lunging forward, I hope and pray I make contact with my target.

But then, suddenly, my arm is grabbed.

My eyes fly open, a scream building... Till I get a good look at the man who has a hold of me.

Wait, what?

"D-D-Detective Silver, what are you doing here?" I blubber, stunned.

He lets go of my arm and the knife clatters to the ground.

With his eyes glued to the glinting metal on the cement floor, the detective shakes his head. "I believe I should be the one asking you that question, Miss Cumberland."

"Yes." I suddenly feel very foolish. "I suppose you should."

Dragging his gaze from the knife to the bloody towel still in my grasp, he inquires, "And what exactly are you doing here all alone in the Lowry barn, with a knife…and a bloody towel?"

"Uh…" I shrug.

Huffing, he continues. "I have to tell you, Jaynie, this doesn't look good. You up here on the property all alone, holding what looks an awful lot like the evidence your boyfriend claims to have discovered this past weekend."

Shit, I am so busted.

And I have no adequate response.

What would I be doing up here all by myself? After all, I hate this place and the detective knows it. Oh, and then there's the inconvenient fact that I just pulled a knife on him. Plus, the bloody towel is still in my hand.

"Shit," I murmur.

"Miss Cumberland?" I venture an upward glance at the detective and he does *not* look happy. "I'm waiting for an explanation."

"I don't know if I have one," I confess.

He lets out a snort. "Then we have a huge problem here, don't we?"

"I'm not sure what you mean," I whisper.

Like he's going to buy that clueless act?

Gently, he slides the towel from my hand. "Tampering with evidence is a crime. You're smart enough to know this, right?"

I avert my eyes. "Yes, I'd assume it'd be an unwise thing to do."

The detective mumbles something I can't make out, and then he says, "You know what carries an even stiffer penalty, though? More than what's standard for simply tampering with evidence?"

Aw, crap, he's on to us.

"What?" I squeak out.

"Actually *manufacturing* said evidence. That, Miss Cumberland, is a felony for which you could receive several years of prison time."

Terrified, I blurt out a tearful, "I'm sorry. I am so, so sorry. I—I just did what I thought I had to, sir."

Detective Silver spends a good thirty seconds peering at me and shaking his head.

Finally, in a soft tone, he says, "Are you confessing to me that *you* planted that evidence?"

Willing to take the fall for Flynn, I tuck in my chin and stare down at the cement floor. "Yep, uh-huh, it was me, all me. Every part of it, besides the phone call Flynn made to you."

"Miss Cumberland." I glance up and the detective is giving me a *yeah, right* look. "I know that's not true," he goes on. "Do you think I didn't see that a vial of blood went missing the day you and Flynn were in my car?"

Crap, he did notice.

Lying to protect Flynn, since I will *always* protect him, I meet Detective Silver's gaze and state emphatically, "Yeah, I figured you'd eventually notice a vial was missing. But I'm the one who took it. Not Flynn, if that's what you're implying."

"No, you didn't take the blood, Jaynie."

"Yes," I insist, "I did. I absolutely took it. You know I'd do anything to keep Allison locked up. I have *far* more motivation than Flynn."

"That may be true." The detective sighs. "But it's also true that Flynn loves you, very deeply from what I've observed."

"He does." My voice cracks. I'm having a hard time keeping up this farce.

"Look, I know you're lying to protect Flynn. But there's no need to. I've already pieced together what probably happened."

"Oh, yeah? What do you think happened?"

The detective then lays his theory out for me, which is pretty spot-on.

He says, "Flynn's coat was lying across the evidence that day in the car. I asked him to cover the blood and the files, remember?"

I nod.

"Well, when one vial went missing, I knew right away he'd grabbed it when he picked up his coat. You didn't touch anything that day, Jaynie. So see, there's no sense in taking the fall for your boyfriend. I've known the truth since day one."

"Why didn't you say anything?" I whisper, truly curious.

The detective is silent for a beat, like he's contemplating something.

Finally, he says, "Believe it or not, kid, I'm on your side. I figured as long as Flynn didn't do anything with the blood, I'd just let it slide. You've both seen enough trouble in your lives. Why add to it over a stupid move?"

I return to my original position of trying to save Flynn. Because he *did* do something with the blood, and this is too big to, as the detective put, let slide.

Flynn's going to have to pay for what he did…unless I can stop it.

"You're wrong on one thing," I throw out.

"What's that, Jaynie?"

"Flynn may have lifted the blood, but I planted the evidence. So you may as well go ahead and charge me, since I committed the bigger crime." My voice cracks again. "Arrest me, Detective Silver." I hold out my hands, wrists up. "Go ahead, I'm ready."

Am I?

No.

But I will go down to save Flynn.

The detective, however, makes no move to cuff me. He stands there, completely quiet, and looking wary. Clearly, he's past the point of buying my false story.

Defeated, I murmur, "I had to try."

"I know."

Resigned that there's no getting out of this mess, I lower my hands and confess. "I just wanted to protect Flynn. I will always try to protect him. At any cost."

"Even if it's to your own detriment, Miss Cumberland?"

The detective isn't trying to be an asshole; he seems to genuinely want to know.

So I tell him the truth. "Yes, it doesn't matter. I'll take the fall for Flynn any day."

Detective Silver bends down. With the edge of the towel he took from me, he picks up the bloodied knife. A few seconds later he's dropping both items into a plastic evidence bag, which he promptly seals.

Gesturing for me to follow, he says, "Come with me, Miss Cumberland."

I expect the book to be thrown at me, but there are no handcuffs placed on me as we begin to walk, no rights read as we leave the Lowry property.

When we reach his car, which is pulled up tight behind mine, I finally flat-out ask, "Am I under arrest?"

"No" is the detective's simple reply.

Our eyes meet, but he quickly turns away. I just stand there and observe as he pops open the trunk of his car and takes out a gas can.

What is he up to now?

I have no idea.

But when he tosses the bloody towel and knife, still in the plastic evidence bag, on the ground, and then starts pouring gasoline all over it, I gasp. "Wait. What are you doing?"

The detective's reply is swift. "I'm destroying these items to protect you and your reckless boyfriend from your own damn selves."

I am speechless. No one ever does stuff like this for us.

As he sets the evidence we planted on fire, ensuring Flynn and I remain safe from being discovered, I stand there, mouth agape.

Seems he really is on our side. We can truly trust him.

"Thank you," I mumble.

"You're welcome," I am told.

Though I am off the hook, I can't deny the person I've become. Good or bad, the fact remains that I was willing to take the fall to protect Flynn. And it doesn't end there. Had the detective not shown up, I probably would have taken that evidence and moved it elsewhere on the property. Then I would've been the one who planted the evidence. I hadn't reached that point yet, but I know now that that's what I would have done.

Because what I told the detective is true—I'll do anything to protect Flynn.

What if Allison got out and went after him, instead of me?

I couldn't let that happen.

And better I fall than him.

It doesn't matter now, though.

The evidence we manufactured is gone, burning up before my eyes.

Chapter Thirty-Five

Flynn

I insist Crick take off, but he wants to stay.

"No, man, I'll be fine, Really, I will," I reiterate when he offers for about the fourth time in as many minutes to remain with me until I know for sure that Jaynie is safe.

He finally agrees to go. "Call me if you need anything," he says.

"You got it."

Once he's gone, I head up to our apartment, where I promptly begin pacing the small space we call home.

"Where are you, Jaynie?" I mutter to the still and heavy air.

I am frustrated and officially out of options. Except for the one I've been avoiding—call the police and report Jaynie as missing.

But just as I'm about to give in and hit 9-1-1 on my cell, I hear a car pulling up out back.

Racing over to the window, I see it's Jaynie, returning with the car and filling me with relief.

"Christ. Thank God she's all right."

I'm down the stairs and out back in no time.

"Jaynie…" I wrap her in my arms the second she's out of the car. "Where the hell were you all day, babe?" I stare into her eyes and brush back a lock of hair. "You didn't answer any of my calls, and I must've made about fifty. Fuck, I was going crazy with worry, sweetheart."

"Flynn, I am so, so sorry," she breathes out.

I hug her again. "Babe, what happened?" I ask.

"I fucked everything up," she chokes out against my shoulder. "I should never have gone back to the Lowry place."

Oh, shit.

"Jaynie, what'd you do? Why in the hell would you go back there?"

"I couldn't let you go down for us," she cries. "Keeping Allison in prison wasn't worth *you* going to jail, Flynn."

Uh-oh, this sounds bad.

I draw back and say quietly, "We should talk about this inside."

We're all alone, but still, the alley is no place for a conversation like this.

Back up in our room, Jaynie proceeds to tell me everything. She reiterates how she couldn't let me go down for planting evidence, and then details how she went to the barn and dug up the towel and the knife.

She tells me how Detective Silver showed up and caught her red-handed, which leaves me muttering, "Fuck, fuck, fuck," as I scrub a hand down my face.

"He figured it all out, Flynn," she says quietly. "Every last bit of it."

"I could've warned you he was coming," I mutter, "if you'd picked up before you got there."

"I had no cell service," she replies, which I know is the truth. "And, besides, it's not like you knew what I was doing."

She's right on that one. Had I known I would've stopped her.

I blow out a breath. "Just thank God you're okay." And then it hits me, the full implications of her story. "Wait." I peer over at her, confused. "How are you even here with me in this apartment? How are you not down at the police station, under arrest? Not that I'm not overjoyed that you *are* here, but *how* are you here?"

"Detective Silver let me go" is Jaynie's easy-going response. Like this happens every day, the police letting criminals go.

"He let you go?" To say I'm in a state of disbelief would be an understatement.

"Yes," she replies.

"Even after he admitted that he knew I stole the blood *and* that he's aware we created fake evidence?" Before she can reply, I add, "Oh, and let's not forget you were tampering with that fake evidence, pretty much right in front of his face."

"Yes, I was," she admits.

"Yet, after all that, he was willing to look away?"

"Yes, Flynn, that's pretty much how it all went down."

"Why?" I ask. "Why let us off the hook like that?"

She shrugs. "I don't know, but let's not question it too much. Let's just be happy we finally have someone in our corner."

Shaking my head, I reply, "That's fine with me. But I'm still shocked. He always claimed to have our backs, and—"

"He definitely does," Jaynie finishes for me.

Arching a brow, I say, "You *do* realize there is one bad thing in all of this, right?"

"That Allison will walk now," she replies. "Yes, I know. But she would've walked anyway, if I'd destroyed the evidence."

"Would you have, though?" I eye her intently, searching for the truth of how far she was willing to go. "Or were you planning on planting that shit somewhere else?"

"I never got that far," she answers, looking sheepish and guilty as hell. "Detective Silver showed up prior to my deciding."

Sighing, I say, "Well, it's over. And it's probably for the best all the way around. It's not like it was real evidence."

"True." Jaynie crosses her arms and shakes her head. "God, though. I hate that there was nothing up there, nothing real, to keep Allison behind bars."

Suddenly feeling more optimistic than I have in ages, probably due to the fact we received a huge break today, I say, "Hey, you never know. Maybe Detective Silver will feel compelled to look around one final time. And maybe something will turn up if he does."

Jaynie then hands me her cell, and says, "Forget about maybes, Flynn. I think we should call him, beg him if we have to, but let's make sure he takes one more look before he closes the case."

Chapter Thirty-Six

Jaynie

We call and ask, but Detective Silver makes no promises one way or the other. He does tell us the usual: "If I decide to go back to the Lowry property, you two will be the first to know."

"Fair enough," Flynn replies.

Exhausted from the day and all that's happened, Flynn and I decide to go to bed early. We're asleep within minutes, but I awake hours later with a start.

Flynn is up in an instant as well. He's that attuned to my night terrors.

"Bad dream?" he asks, propping himself up on one elbow.

"Not this time," I reply. "There was no dream, actually. None at all. But I still felt..." I search for the right words to explain what exactly has me so uneasy that I woke from a dead sleep.

"I don't know, Flynn," I whisper. "I just suddenly felt like you weren't lying here next to me. Like"—my voice trembles—"like you had left and I was all alone again."

I touch his cheek, his nose, his chin, just to verify he's really here.

"Babe…" He leans in and presses his lips to mine. "I'm here. And I'll always be here. We'll never again be apart."

"Yeah, but we could've been," I say, sighing. "If Detective Silver wasn't so kind, we would've both been arrested."

"But he is kind," Flynn assures me as he rolls on top of me, a little breathless. "And neither of us is in any kind of trouble."

He then smothers me in kisses, a successful attempt to distract me from my unnecessary worries.

"Yes," I breathe out, my pulse racing as Flynn deposits feathery kisses along my neck. "We may not be in that bad kind of trouble," I say. "But you're going to find yourself in a really good kind of trouble"—I gasp—"if you keep kissing me like this."

"Duly noted," he murmurs.

The intensity of those kisses is amped up, each one hotter than the kiss before. But then it's too much…all the damn clothes, that is. I need Flynn, and I need him now.

Tugging at the hem of his tee, I murmur, "Take this off."

He complies and then, nodding to his boxer-clad lower body, asks in a teasing tone, "You want me to leave these on, though, right?"

"Are you kidding me?" I scoff.

I slide my hand inside his boxers and that pretty much puts an end to any additional silly talk of leaving on clothes that clearly need to come off.

A minute later Flynn is back on me…and then he's in me. A few minutes more and I am crying out his name, along with declarations of my undying love.

This is good. This is better than we've been in a long time. This joining of our bodies doesn't feel rushed. It's not what it's been these past couple months—frenzied, desperate.

Our joining this night speaks of one thing only—love.

Chapter Thirty-Seven

Detective Silver

As I drive up the steep hill that leads to the Lowry property, the shovel I stowed in the trunk before I left the precinct clinking away, I have to ask myself one question: Why am I so hell-bent on helping Flynn and Jaynie? It's not like I know them, not really. But here I am, at the Lowry property once more.

Really, what the hell?

I've already jeopardized my career by letting those two get away with planting fake evidence. I even went so far as to cover up what they did. Yet I'm back on this property at their request to search one final time before the Debbie Canfield case has to be closed for good.

As I make my way to the pole barn Jaynie and Flynn refer to as the 'work barn'—that damn clanking shovel finally silenced since it now rests in my grasp—I think back to my own reckless youth.

Ah, therein I know I'll find the answer as to why I am so committed to helping these kids.

I never had a bad home life, but I was a rebel at heart. I butted heads with my parents almost constantly. Caught up in the early '90s grunge rock movement, I fancied myself at the time the next Kurt Cobain, or maybe even an Eddie Vedder.

Only problem was I had no band.

But I sure was determined to find one.

One day, after having no luck in my Podunk West Virginia town, I took off, hitching rides across the country until I ended up in Seattle.

Where it all began, I thought.

Being the naïve seventeen-year-old that I was at that time, I was sure I'd find my future bandmates on the streets of the Emerald City. It was like I'd found my way to a grunge rock Oz.

What a fool I was, I think, shaking my head.

Three days of hanging out in Pioneer Square with all the homeless was all it took for me to open my eyes. I realized then that the kids who were there weren't looking to make music; they were looking to survive. I saw things no kid should ever see. And by day number four, I was calling my mom, crying and begging to come home.

My understanding mom, just happy I was alive and well, sent me a bus ticket back to West Virginia. The whole ride home I kept counting my blessings for what I had been so stupid to ever take for granted. Things like a roof over my head, plenty to eat, and parents who, though we fought, loved me.

And that's it. That's why I have a soft spot for Jaynie and Flynn. I see them as two kids, not so different from who I once was. But they've not been nearly as fortunate. Sadly, life's dealt them a bad hand, until recently. Though I don't think they always see it, they've been thriving since escaping the Lowry house.

But what'll happen to those kids if Allison gets out of prison?

She may leave them alone, sure. But then again, she may not.

Why take a chance?

That's why I'm here and ready to search once more for something, *anything* to keep that wicked girl behind bars.

Where to start, where to start, I ask myself as I walk into the barn. I stop and look around.

The one thing that's been bothering me since Flynn called that weekend is the loose cement slab. Why would a section of the flooring in a new structure come loose so soon after construction?

There's no good reason, unless it was tampered with.

That's where I decide to search, so I start walking again and head straight over to the area Flynn told me about.

Finding the right area is easy, seeing as Jaynie never moved the piece of cement back in to place.

Standing there, the hole in the ground that Flynn dug stares back at me, daring me to dig farther, much farther than where he stopped.

I take a deep breath.

And then I start to dig.

I dig and dig, going far beyond where Flynn once hid food. Deeper than where the fake evidence was placed as well.

I continue to dig and dig, until I finally hit something solid.

Interesting...

Dropping to my knees—to hell with my recently dry-cleaned suit—I fish around in the soft earth with my hands. And that's when I find something.

I lift the item up.

"Damn," I murmur.

It's a bone—a human one, from what I can tell.

I continue to dig, uncovering another, then another...

Chapter Thirty-Eight

Flynn

On Saturday, Jaynie and I drive up to Morgantown to visit with Mandy and the twins. Josh is working a double, so it's just the five of us. Like old times.

Inspired by those old times, we take Cody and Callie to a local park so we can play the kids' games they love so very much. The games they choose are the ones we used to play up in the fields by the Lowry house, games like Tag and Hide and Seek.

"Stay within the limits of the park," Mandy tells the twins before we begin our first game, Hide and Seek.

"Okay, Mom," Callie and Cody echo back as they run off in opposite directions.

I've been designated 'it' for this first game, so after counting to one hundred, I open my eyes and begin to search.

I find Jaynie first, hidden behind a swing set. "Lame," I tell her.

"Eh." She shrugs. "Maybe I wanted you to find me first."

That earns her a peck on the cheek.

Next up, with Jaynie's help, I locate Mandy. She's curled up in one of those plastic tube slides.

"These are for kids," I say to her when she has to crawl out, all awkward-like. "They're clearly not designed for adults."

"Pfft," she snorts. "Admit it, Flynn. It was a pretty good hiding place."

"Not that good," I say in a teasing tone. "I found you, right?"

She pushes me away. "Shut up. You only found me with Jaynie's help."

"I'll ignore that comment," I say as the three of us share a laugh.

Next, on my own, I find Cody.

He's hidden behind a big tree. It's not a very good hiding spot, but I tell him otherwise to build his confidence.

"I pick the best-est hiding place *ever*," he says, puffing out his chest. "Don't I, Flynnie?"

"You sure do, kiddo," I reply.

Cody then promptly gives away his sister.

Running over to a thick growth of shrubs, he pulls back the branches and informs a crouching Callie, "Did you see where I was hiding, Callie? Flynnie tell me I picked a good spot."

"Cody!" Callie yells as she stands up and brushes off her knees. "You just gave me away, you jerk."

"Hey, no name-calling," Mandy chastises.

Since the kids are all wound up, we adults call for a break before the next game begins.

"It'll give the kids some time to cool down," Mandy says to me and Jaynie in a low voice as she hands the twins money for a nearby ice cream vendor.

Once they run off, the three of us sit down at a picnic bench, one where we have a good view of them.

"This day is really turning out to be fun," Mandy remarks, smiling over at us.

"It is," I agree. "And it's really good for the twins, a reminder of the old times, but only the good ones."

Jaynie interjects, "Hey, that reminds *me* of something. I have something for you, Mandy."

Mandy appears curious right away. "What is it?" she asks.

Jaynie leans forward and fishes out a folded piece of parchment from the back pocket of her jeans. It's the card the twins made for Mandy last summer.

"I meant to give this to you a long time ago," she says, holding out the card. "I originally found it back in the fall, hidden away in the work barn."

Mandy takes the card and reads it. From the tears gathering in her eyes, it's clear she's touched by the sweet sentiments the twins wrote long ago.

"Thank you for saving it for me," she says softly when she's done reading.

"I knew you would want it," Jaynie says. "I'd forgotten about it back in the fall, but, luckily, I came across it last weekend when we were up at the work barn…"

Jaynie trails off, and we all fall silent. No one wants to bring up the subject of our failure to find evidence against Allison. It means there will never be justice for Debbie. Plus, Allison will be out of prison soon, free to do as she chooses.

I'm about to say something to lighten the rapidly growing somber mood, but just then my cell phone rings. We don't get many calls, so it's no surprise when Jaynie turns to me and asks, "Who the heck could that be?"

Peering down at the screen, I murmur, "It's Detective Silver."

"Answer it," she says excitedly. "Hurry, Flynn, before it goes to voice mail."

I do as Jaynie asks, and Detective Silver starts speaking right away. I listen, expecting the worst—that he found no evidence at the

Lowry place and that it's all over.

But then, as he goes on and on, his words paint a picture of a different outcome, one that's making me smile like a lunatic.

"What is it?" Jaynie grabs my arm. "What's he saying that's making you so ridiculously happy, Flynn?"

Mandy chimes in, "Yeah, what's going on?"

"Good news," I mouth to the girls.

And it is. It's the kind of news that leaves me feeling that, for the first time in a long time, the world just might be on our side.

Chapter Thirty-Nine

Jaynie

*A*llison Lowry remains in prison.

Detective Silver's call, informing us that Debbie Canfield's skeleton was found in the work barn, right where Flynn and I planted evidence, makes sure of that.

Wow, it was there all along, everything we needed. We just hadn't dug deeply enough.

No matter, the case is solved.

The coroner determines that Debbie was strangled, and the early clues point to Allison. And then, to everyone's surprise, some very damning evidence is discovered.

A diary was apparently buried with Debbie, far below where her bones were. The book doesn't belong to the missing girl, however. It belongs to Allison, and it contains her own detailed account of how she planned to get rid of Debbie.

The find is as good as a confession, and our former tormentor is charged with murder. A trial date is set, but by the end of the summer

Allison confesses, eliminating the need for a trial. She's sentenced to life in prison, with no possibility for parole.

A few weeks later, the Lowry house and both barns are condemned. The property itself is slated to become a nature preserve and park. Flynn and I are happy with those developments, especially the idea of a park. From that point on, we closely monitor all progress to make sure it really happens.

And it does. The barns are torn down immediately, just not the house.

"It's supposed to be demolished by October first," Flynn informs me.

Curious as to how things look up there now, I suggest we drive over to Forsaken to see for ourselves.

We're in a good mood on the way over, both of us happy that soon *all* the reminders of our suffering will be gone.

"This feels good," I say to Flynn after we arrive at the Lowry property.

"It does," he agrees with a smile.

We walk up the driveway and stop once we reach the house where we were once held captive.

"Knowing everything up here is about to be obliterated feels *so* right," I murmur.

He hands me a rock. "Let's make it feel even better."

We proceed to throw rocks at the house, just like Jenny did in the movie *Forrest Gump*. And also like in the movie, sometimes there are just not enough rocks.

Afterward, we hike up to the cliffs and our secret place in the woods. They're the only good places on the property, and we're both thrilled they'll remain untouched, both designated as parts of the preserve.

"After all, this is the place where we fell in love," I say to Flynn under the ever-watchful ancient pines.

"And this is the place where I first kissed you," he adds.

He steps in front of me and takes my face in his hands.

"Kiss me now," I whisper.

He does. He kisses me now, today, in this moment.

"I love you, Jaynie-bird," he murmurs against my lips.

"I love you too, Flynn O'Neill."

We spend the next several minutes kissing, just kissing. We're better at it than we were back then, because we know—we just know each other so incredibly well.

When we break apart, I declare, "This is like the end of an era and the start of a whole new beginning."

Chuckling, he remarks, "Seems like we've had a lot of those, both endings and beginnings."

"Maybe more than our fair share," I agree. "But"—I rise to my tiptoes and kiss him on his cheek—"I have a feeling this new beginning is going to be the absolute best."

"I think so too," he agrees.

"Let's seal it with another kiss," I murmur, my soul humming with renewed hope.

"Let's," Flynn says.

We then do exactly that, because in every ending there is a chance for a new beginning.

And this one is ours.

Epilogue I

Flynn

It's been a while since that day on the cliffs—six years, to be exact. And the declaration we made that our new beginning that day was going to be the best... Well, that declaration has come to fruition. Our new life together—the life we started living after we truly put the past behind us—is the very best.

It's so good these days, this life. No, wait—it's *great*.

Jaynie and I now live up in Morgantown. We rent a three-bedroom apartment that feels like a mansion, and we're saving to buy a house. Nothing fancy, just a place to call our own.

We moved up from Lawrence a few years ago so Jaynie could finish her studies at WVU. Oh, and so I could get started on mine.

We're done with school now, though, and both of us are gainfully employed, working in our dream careers, actually.

How cool is that?

Jaynie is a counselor and special investigator, but not for the state foster care system. She works with kids, just as she always planned to do—deeply troubled kids, in fact—but she does so with a non-profit organization, one that vehemently stands by its mission statement to help and protect children who have been left behind or have been mistreated in any way.

I should mention here that we're still in touch with Bill Delmont. He owns two sandwich shops now, one located right here in Morgantown. That's important to the details of our life now, but more on that later.

Bill's the same as he always was. That means he's still helping kids who are over eighteen and out of the system. He gives them a chance at a better life. Just last week, Jaynie sent him a runaway who needed help, a kid who was living on the streets of Morgantown, too old for foster care, but too young to make it on his own.

Bill hired the kid on the spot and he now works at the same sandwich shop we once worked in and lived above.

But back to my and Jaynie's current lives...

As mentioned, I now have a degree. And it's in teaching.

That's right, I actually followed through on the plan I devised that day long ago when I was working construction.

I currently teach a class of forty eager-to-learn fifth graders. And man, I love it.

Speaking of kids, it wasn't all school and the prospect of future work that lured Jaynie and me up to Morgantown. Another reason we made the move was to be closer to the twins. After Mandy and Josh ran off and got married, and then officially adopted Cody and Callie, we knew the twins would definitely be staying with them. Jaynie and I decided we didn't want to miss out on watching them grow up.

And we haven't.

The twins are fifteen now. And, wow, all I can say is that they're a handful. In a good way, of course.

Callie is a blast. She makes me laugh when I think of her rebellious heart. I don't know if Mandy would agree, though. Callie's been driving her crazy lately. From what I've heard, she's trying to persuade her mom to let her date some sixteen-year-old skateboard dude.

Mandy doesn't approve of him, but that's no surprise. They butt heads a lot, since Callie is like a mini-Mandy.

The skateboarder is a decent dude, though. I know this because you bet your ass I vetted him. Josh did too, but he's a little bit of a pushover when it comes to the kids. I know that if I give my stamp of approval on the skateboarder dude, Mandy will come around. I will, but I'm going to let the little princess Callie sweat it out a little first.

Cody is also doing great. He finally found his strength—making music. I should've seen it coming, from that day long ago when Jaynie and I taught him math with colored dowels. All he really wanted to do that day was use those dowels as drumsticks. He made an awful racket back then, but he sure does make beautiful music now. He plays all the time too, often filling his family home with electric guitar riffs.

I have to laugh.

I bet Josh rues the day he bought Cody his own guitar. But then again, probably not. When Cody and Josh play together, which they do now quite a bit, they sound incredible. Josh knows it too. That's why he's promised to take Cody out with him when he plays some gigs this summer. Mandy gave them the go-ahead, but only if Cody picks up some extra shifts at the Morgantown Delmont Sandwich Shop.

And we're back to that—the other piece of info I promised you a while back. Mandy partnered with Bill a couple years ago, and when he opened the shop up here he gave it to her to run.

Funny how life turns out sometimes, right?

Mandy was the one who first connected us with Bill, and here she is running his store.

Full circle and all that.

I guess I should share with you what happened to Mrs. Lowry and Allison, though I'd just as well not. But those two people who caused so much pain, you must be wondering what became of them.

Well, I'm pleased to report that Mrs. Lowry is still behind bars, and will be for a long time.

And Allison, well she's gone. Yeah, you read that right. The girl is dead. She was stabbed during a prison fight four years ago. Sorry, but I have to confess that no tears were shed for that one.

Okay, enough about those two. Let's return to the here and now and all the positive shit that's been happening in our lives.

Like, did I mention Jaynie and I got married this past weekend?

What? No?

Well, we did.

Jaynie and I exchanged our vows of devotion under the stars, on the cliff that remains our special place.

A reverend who's a friend of Bill's officiated the late evening ceremony. Josh was my best man, and Mandy was Jaynie's matron of honor. Callie was our flower girl, and Cody, the ring bearer. Bill and Detective Silver came to the wedding, and Crick, sitting front and center, stood and spoke a few words, adding his own special flair.

All in all, our tiny wedding was perfect. And afterward we partied at the sandwich shop.

Man, I love married life. Though sometimes I can't believe Jaynie is really my wife.

How did I ever get so lucky?

My cell beeps, interrupting my rambling thoughts.

Hey, it's Jaynie, texting me, telling me she has something important to tell me…

Epilogue II

Jaynie

Flynn meets me back at our apartment, but this is not where I want to give him my good news.

I grab his hand and say, "Come on. Let's take a ride."

"Where to?" he asks.

"That's a surprise, along with my news." I tug on his arm. "Hurry, Flynn, hurry."

"You're killing me, Jaynie," he jokes.

But he follows me, just as I always follow him. That hasn't changed.

When we hit the interstate, I head south out of Morgantown. Flynn tries again to elicit some info from me, but to no avail.

"Can you at least give me a clue as to where we're going?" he asks.

"Nope," I maintain. "I told you it's a surprise, just like my news."

God, Flynn is going to be shocked by what I have to tell him.

He gives up, mumbling a defeated, "Okay, okay."

When we finally come to a stop, we're in Lawrence, down by the river, not far from the sandwich shop.

"Are we going to the park?" Flynn correctly guesses.

"Yes, we are."

It's a drizzly spring afternoon, not unlike the day I first met Flynn. And like the day I met him, he still takes my breath away. At twenty-four, he is all man now, and more stunning than ever.

Hand in hand, we stroll down to the river's edge. When we stop on the muddy banks, I turn to him and say, "This is the exact spot where I dragged my ass out of the water all those years ago. You know," I add softly, "the night I jumped from the cliff."

Flynn moves to stand behind me so we're both facing the water with the same vantage point. With his chin resting on my shoulder, he says, "Right here exactly, huh?"

I nod once. "Yes. And I've viewed this riverbank, since that day, as the place of my re-birth. That's why I wanted to be *here* when I give you my news."

"Jaynie..."

An edge of worry has crept into Flynn's voice, but there's no need for concern.

I hasten to get that across to him when I say, "What I'm about to tell you is something good. It's the happy kind of news—the *very* happy kind."

"Jaynie, please, just tell me," he begs.

I lower his hands to my abdomen. I can't keep him in suspense a minute more.

"Flynn," I begin, "this is where I was given a chance at a new life. And this is where you should learn about another new life, a life you helped create."

He sucks in a breath. "What are you saying, Jaynie?" His voice is uneven, but filled with so much hope.

"What do you think I'm saying?" I whisper.

He turns me so I'm facing him and places his hands on my

tummy from this new angle. He then asks, "Are you… Are you…?" He lowers his eyes. "I'm afraid to say the words. I'm afraid this might all be a dream. I'm afraid I'll wake up and none of this will be real."

"It's all real," I whisper.

He looks up at me, and God, the hope and yearning in his soft gray eyes tugs at my heart. "It's really what I'm thinking?"

"Yes." I nod like crazy.

Flynn deserves this so much. And I'm elated that I can give him what I never thought possible. I was told long ago that I may never have kids. I thought at the time it was true, so much so that Flynn and I gave up birth control years ago. For a while, not all that long ago, we even tried.

But nothing ever happened.

Until now.

Beaming, I say the words I never thought would pass my lips. "I'm pregnant, Flynn. I'm really pregnant. I didn't want to say anything for a few weeks. You know…just in case. But I'm twelve weeks along now, and I had another doctor's appointment just the other da—"

"I'm going with you to *all* of those from now on," he interjects.

"Yes, yes, of course. I was just afraid, at first. I didn't want to get your hopes up. But after what they told me last visit, I want you there with me every step of the way from here on out."

"What'd they say at your last visit?" Flynn wants to know, looking suddenly worried.

"Nothing bad," I assure him. "Everything looks good, in fact. Our baby is developing on schedule and appears to be perfectly healthy."

"Jaynie…" Flynn swipes away a tear, and then another. "Don't worry, these are happy tears," he assures me.

"I already knew that," I tell him.

These moments I've experienced by the river bank, they define my life. When my rebirth occurred, half a dozen years ago, I was given a fresh start, a new life. And now today, as we speak of an anxiously awaited birth, I get the sense this is going down in the annals of history as the happiest day of that new life.

I turn out to be wrong, though.

The happiest day of my life is the day I give birth to a seven-pound, four-ounce little boy, whom Flynn and I name Galen, in honor of the little brother Flynn lost.

That day is the best, by far, for the both of us.

It's also the day we learn that sometimes even the saddest of stories have the happiest of endings.

The End

About the Author

S.R. Grey is an Amazon Top 100 and a #1 Barnes & Noble Best Selling Author. She is the author of the highly popular Judge Me Not series, the new Promises series, the Inevitability duology, A Harbour Falls Mystery trilogy, and the Laid Bare series of novellas. Ms. Grey's works have appeared on several Amazon Bestseller lists, including the Top 100 multiple times, as well as #1 on Barnes & Noble Bestselling Nook Books.

Ms. Grey has a hilarious new Sports Romance/Romantic Comedy coming out this winter. Follow and visit the following sites to stay up-to-date on a Blurb Reveal, a Cover Reveal (featuring an über-hot model), and publication specifics.

S.R. Grey Facebook:
www.facebook.com/SRGrey

Author Website:
srgrey.com

Sign up for S.R. Grey's exclusive-content newsletter and never miss an update, cover reveal, or release:
mad.ly/signups/106801/join

S.R. Grey on Twitter:
twitter.com/AuthorSRGrey

S.R. Grey Goodreads Author page:
www.goodreads.com/author/show/6433082.S_R_Grey

S.R. Grey on Instagram:
instagram.com/authorsrgrey#

Read the prologue of the award-winning and top-ranking *I Stand Before You*, the first novel in S.R. Grey's best-selling Judge Me Not series.

I Stand Before You

Prologue
Chase

I lean my head back against the headrest, crank the passenger window down the rest of the way. The June night air rustles through my hair, reminding me I desperately need a trim. I run my fingers through the strands, chasing the path of the breeze.

My grandmother likes to lecture that I shouldn't have hair sticking out at odd angles, strands curling at the nape of my neck.

"You're such a handsome young man, Chase," Grandma Gartner said just this morning, *tsk*ing when I sat down for breakfast. "You look so much like your father did when he was your age. But, you know, *he* always kept *his* hair short and tidy." And then there was a pause, a long, dramatic sigh. She set down a plate of eggs—over easy—in front of me. "My poor Jack. God rest his soul." My grandmother crossed herself.

Her poor Jack, my father with the short and tidy hair—dead and gone.

I thought: *I am not my dad, Gram. He failed us, he gave up on us.* But the words never passed my lips. And they never will. Hearing them would only hurt my grandmother's feelings and she's too good to hear the angry thoughts poisoning my polluted mind. So I keep all that shit locked deep inside.

This morning was no different. I kept things light, said something like, "The girls like my hair like this, Gram. Got to keep the ladies happy, ya know."

Then I ducked and waited for the inevitable swat with the dish towel. But it never came. Instead, the lines in my grandmother's face deepened.

"You don't need to be concerning yourself with keeping ladies happy, young man. You're only twenty. Messing with women at your age will only lead to trouble."

I knew what she meant this morning, and I know it now too. She's worried I'll end up getting some girl pregnant. Then I'll be fucked, well and good. But I'm always careful, take the necessary precautions. Besides, it isn't my womanizing ways that's becoming a problem. If only. No, unfortunately, it's my ever-growing dependency on drugs—something my grandmother would never suspect—that has me worried these days.

These days... Yeah, right. More like these blurry, fucked-up segments of time.

Sighing, I roll the window up just enough to lean my head against the cool glass. *What am I going to do?* I silently ask myself.

What I really need to do is get the hell out of this tiny Ohio farm town I landed back in two years ago. I'm spinning my wheels here in Harmony Creek, hanging with a bad crowd. Problem is I have no plan, no money either. Drugs are my escape and have been for quite a while. My priorities are all fucked up. My life, it's upside down. Every day it seems like getting high—and staying that way—is my only goal. I want to stop—believe me I do—but I don't think I know how to anymore.

A lump forms in my throat at this thought, but I swallow it down. "Hey," I say to Tate, who is driving. "Let's get out of this town."

Tate Cody, my friend...and my partner in crime in everything wild and crazy these days—women, drugs, drinking, fighting—you name it, we do it. And if we're not doing it nowadays, chances are we've done it at least once over the past couple of years. We've yet to slow down; we live on the edge.

I sometimes wonder when we'll fall.

"What do you think we're doing, Chase, my man?"

I take in and process Tate's reply, while he lifts a bottle of cheap gin to his lips and hits the gas. And for this one long, tortuous drawn-out second, I can't make a distinction between what I asked Tate and what I was only thinking. I panic, assuming my partner in crime's response is to let me know it's finally happening, we're really falling.

But then Tate adds, "I'm getting us out of here as fast as I can," and I breathe a little easier. He just means we're leaving Harmony Creek. Not falling, after all. *Shit, I need to ease up on the drugs.*

I glance out the window, and though it's dark I can see we're heading east, nearing the state line. Soon we'll be out of Ohio completely, and in the neighboring state of Pennsylvania. That's where we're supposed to hook up with two girls tonight. They're from New Castle, and we're meeting at a lake across the state line.

I don't really care about all that, though. What I'd really rather do is keep on going. Hop on Interstate 80 and clock the miles to Jersey. Better yet, Tate and I could go farther. We could drive our asses straight into New York-fucking-City. Now that would be sweet.

So while Tate barrels down a back road the police rarely patrol—until you get into Pennsylvania, that is—I pretend we're leaving Harmony Creek for good. No looking back, no regrets, just flying the fuck out of this lame-ass small town.

And speaking of flying, I'm flying a bit now too, feeling fine, baby, fine. I close my eyes so I can savor the s-l-o-w creep of numbness that cocoons me like a warm and fuzzy blanket.

I feel nothing, yet I feel everything.

My skin tingles a little, but when I touch my hand to my face it feels detached, like these parts of my body belong to two different people, neither of them me. That thought makes me happy, escape is exactly what I crave.

Needless to say, I've smoked—a lot—and not just weed. But it's the pills I swallowed a while ago that are starting to wrap me up and spin me the fuck out.

A bottle hits the back of my hand and my eyes fly open. Shit, I forgot I am not alone in this car.

"Drink, fucker," Tate urges.

I take the gin, despite the fact I can barely see straight. *No* isn't part of my vocabulary when I'm like this. And, sadly, more often than not, this is exactly how I am. This is who I am becoming: Chase Gartner, burgeoning drug addict.

As per most nights, Tate and I stopped at Kyle's before embarking on *this* night's little adventure. Kyle Tanner supplies us with more drugs than we could ever hope for. And the quality is always top notch. Kyle takes a certain kind of pride in dealing only primo product. But you'd never guess such a thing if you saw the rundown shithole he lives in.

Our dealer resides on the *other* side of town, over by the closed-down glass factory, in a clapboard house he shares with his meth-addicted dad. Lately, going there has been a contradiction of emotions for me. I love and hate concurrently when Tate and I cross over the railroad tracks that mark the end of the safe neighborhoods of Harmony Creek. Then, I vacillate between love and hate as I watch the Sparkle Mart grocery store appear…then disappear. I lean a little more towards hate when we reach the run-down apartment building where the junkies hang out, where their emaciated bodies lean lazily against the dirty brick exterior.

I sure as fuck don't want to end up there, God, no. But maybe I'm powerless to stop my downward spiral. Lord knows, by the time we start down the long dirt road that leads to Kyle's place, I crave and I want. And love trumps hate by that point. Even the junkies seem less scary. So we go…and we go…and we keep going back.

Tate tells me the road to Kyle's house is the road to salvation. *Salvation, my ass.* I'd be more inclined to say Tate and I are traveling a path to hell. We're in the express lane to damnation, and one step closer to burning every time we travel down that fucking dirt road. I know it, he knows it, but do we ever do anything to stop? Do we try to crawl out of the hole we're wallowing in? No, never.

In fact, Tate wants us to delve in deeper—start selling. He says we'll make, at the minimum, enough money to help pay for the copious amounts of shit we ingest…snort…smoke. Yeah, we do it all, everything short of needles. I somehow know if I ever cross *that* line, there will be no going back.

But I'm considering the selling thing, albeit for a different reason than my friend. Tate hopes to eventually make enough cash to buy his own wheels. He hates borrowing the piece of shit we're currently in—his mom's old, rusted Ford Focus. I just want to make enough money to buy a ticket out of this place. The little bit I earn painting people's houses, picking up construction work here and there—it's not adding up fast enough for my liking.

Hell, I still live at my grandmother's farmhouse out on Cold Springs Lane. Granted, I recently fixed up the little apartment above the detached garage, moved from a bedroom in the main house to an area not too much larger. But that little apartment provides privacy, and that's what I need. I am no longer a teenager, like when I first moved back two years ago. That's why I want, more than anything, to just get the fuck out of here. I'm thinking the money I make selling will make escape a reality, not just some pipe dream. No pun intended.

I raise the bottle of gin to my lips and tip it back. Alcohol heats my throat. "I think I'm going to take Kyle up on his offer," I say after I swallow the burn, the resulting grimace distorting my voice. "I need the money and it's going to take forever to earn it legit."

"You're making the right decision, my friend," Tate replies as he reaches over to take back the bottle.

Whoa... My vision turns wonky. There are three overlapping filmy images of my friend, and then just two.

"It's all about the numbers, man," two filmy Tates tell me.

I tell myself I need to slow down, and then I say to Tate, "That it is." I squeeze my eyes shut to keep from swaying in my seat. "That it is," I repeat.

The irony is that I once had money. Well, my family did, enough that my parents had a trust fund set up for me. Not a big one, mind you, but enough that it would've allowed for me to go to a decent college, get set up in a new city, shit like that.

I have no idea what my future holds nowadays, but I know it's been tainted by my past.

Back when I was around eight my parents moved from this town out to Las Vegas. My dad, who'd been successfully building houses here for a while, started a similar construction business out in Nevada. The timing was right, the stars aligned. We caught magic in the early days of the housing boom. Everything was golden and money poured in. It was happy times. For a while.

During those good times, Mom got pregnant. She gave me a little brother named Will that I still love like crazy and miss every fucking day. We used to talk on the phone all the time, but now I'm lucky if I get a two-word text from my little bro. I suppose when you're eleven years old—and haven't seen your big brother in two years—memories become a little hazy.

That's another thing the extra money from selling drugs will help with: I'll have enough funds to fly out to Vegas to see Will. Or I can just buy him a ticket to come here. As it is my mom, Abby, barely makes enough to get by out there.

But, like I said before, it wasn't always that way. In the early years, my father's construction company grew and thrived, so much so that I once entertained dreams of taking over the business. I used to imagine following in my father's footsteps, as sons are apt to do.

One afternoon, when I was about thirteen, I told my dad I wanted to build homes, same as he did. I showed him some sketches, just some basic designs and floor plans I'd thrown together. My dad was impressed. And not the false kind of fawning parents often try to sell to their kids. No, my drawings truly floored Jack Gartner. I could tell he couldn't believe his eldest son possessed that kind of crazy talent. He told me I should aim high, the sky was the limit. My sketches were incredible, he said, especially for my age. I could be an architect if I wanted, design skyscrapers even.

I had no reason not to believe him.

When you're thirteen you think you can have it all. Life hasn't roughed you up so very much…yet. At least it hadn't for me. So I told my father I'd do both—I would design the skyscrapers, and then I'd build them. My buildings would sell like hotcakes, and I'd be as rich as Donald Trump. No, richer even.

"The sky's the limit," I said, echoing my father's words back to him.

Dad smiled and patted me on the back.

Jack Gartner wasn't patronizing me, he truly believed in my possibility. "You have talent, Chase," he said. "Just don't ever lose yourself. If you can stay true to your dream…to who you are…then you'll do more than fly. Someday you'll soar."

Yeah, right. I sure am soaring at the moment, but I have a feeling this isn't what Dad had in mind.

Tate tries to pass the bottle back to me, but my mood has dampened. The pills, along with the memories, are doing a fucking number on my emotions. I'm sad one minute, reflective the next, mad at everything, contemplative over nothing. I guess I am officially fucked up.

I push the bottle away, harder than necessary, and clear liquid sloshes over the side. "Asshole," Tate mutters.

"Sorry," I say.

Do I really mean it? No, it's just a word, an empty string of letters. Empty, like me.

I tune Tate out. I am high as fuck and lost in my mind. We idle at a swinging red light hanging over an empty, dark stretch of road, and I sit waiting on an imaginary red light in my head, one on memory-fucking-lane.

When I blink, both lights turn green...

My dad started taking me to work the summer I showed him the drawings. I learned how to wire a home, how to put in plumbing, how to lay insulation. And that was just the beginning. I used to watch how my dad talked to the guys. He treated them with respect, and in turn they went the extra mile for him. It was all "Yes sir, Mr. Gartner," "Consider it done, Jack."

When I turned fourteen, my dad bought me a drafting table, a bunch of fancy software too. The kind real architects use, or so he said. I practiced all the time, got pretty damn good. I was building my wings, you see, preparing to fly.

Will was only five, but damn if that kid didn't love to sit around and watch me sketch. For him, I'd draw all kinds of ridiculous structures.

"Dwaw me a house, Chasey," he asked this one day.

I laughed while I tousled his blond hair. I remember the fine strands looked so light in the sunlit room. Hell, they were almost white. "All right, buddy, what kind do you want?"

"A house like a tweeeee," Will sing-song replied, green eyes innocent and wide as he focused on the sketch pad I'd picked up from my desk.

I readied a colored pencil and asked for clarification, "Okay, a tree house, right?"

"No-o-o." Will shook his little head vociferously. "A house that *is* a twee, Chasey."

"Aha, got it," I said.

And I did. I drew Will a tree house shaped exactly like a tree, big, sturdy, loaded down with bushy branches. The leaves I shaded in the color of my brother's eyes. I sketched a door at the base of the trunk, then drew a Will-sized truck and parked it under a low-lying branch. After I finished with some final shading, I held the drawing up for my brother to see.

Will's house looked like one of those tree houses in the commercials with the elves and the cookies, only this one I'd drawn was far better. There was a lot more detail, and I'd drawn the tree in 2-D. In among the branches and the leaves all the rooms were in cross-section, done up in varying shades of blue, Will's favorite color. I also made certain every last blue-shaded 2D-room overflowed with toys.

Will threw his arms around my neck and told me he loved his *twee house*. Then, he leaned back and told me he loved *me* even more.

He gave me a kiss on my cheek. That shit always touched my heart, choked me up a little. "I love you too, buddy," was about all I could say as I held on to a little boy who meant the world to me.

Things are never bad when love is abundant. I thought it would stay that way forever, I did. A home filled with love, a happy family, just a good and easy life.

Man, was I ever wrong.

Shortly after I turned seventeen my world began to crumble. The bottom fell out of the housing market. The wave everyone was riding touched the surf and crashed. My dad's business was one of the first to fail. He had overextended himself; all our assets were mortgaged. He made ridiculous deals, attempting to keep us afloat, but his efforts proved futile. We sunk faster than a stone.

I sold the fancy architect software on eBay, the drafting table too. I gave the money to my parents, but it was merely a drop in the bucket compared to what we owed. I watched my once-vibrant dad turn into a shadow of the man he once was. My mom, always so young-looking and pretty, developed dark circles under her eyes— from crying, worrying, not being able to sleep. She even tried her hand at the casinos, we were that fucking desperate. But everyone knows gambling is a loser's game. The house always wins in the end.

One night, my mom was at one of those casinos. It wasn't the first time she'd spent hours and hours away, trying to win back what we'd lost. She came out ahead a little here and there, but it was never enough, never enough.

Will had fallen asleep early that night, so my dad and I were more or less alone. He asked me if I was hungry. When I nodded slowly, reluctant to reveal just how ravenous I really was and cause my father any additional undue guilt, he sighed, picked up the phone, and ordered a bunch of Chinese take-out.

I swear I smelled that food before the delivery man even pulled up to the house. Beef Chow Mein, General Tso's chicken, Hot and Sour soup, and eggrolls, the first real meal I'd eaten in weeks. And even though my dad and I had to sit on the floor—our furniture had been repossessed days earlier—I savored every fucking bite.

Afterward, my dad said he had somewhere to go. There was something he had to do. Would I keep an eye on Will?

"Sure," I told him while shoving white take-out cartons with little metal handles— leftovers I'd saved for Will and Mom—into the fridge.

With my father gone, I had nothing to do. Our TVs were gone, the stereos too. Video games? Forget it. Those were among the first things to go. So, I wandered around the house barefoot, padding around on neglected hardwood floors. I trudged from one empty room to the next.

Then I took a minute to look in on Will.

My little brother slept on an air mattress in the middle of his now-barren room. The *twee house* sketch, the only thing left on his four stark walls, had fallen. It lay abandoned on the floor, close to Will's hand, close to where his little arm was dangling off the side of the mattress. To me, it looked as if my brother was subconsciously reaching for the drawing. Three years had passed since I'd drawn Will's tree house—and I'd sketched hundreds of other things for him since that sunny day—but that particular piece of made-with-love art was still my brother's favorite. I think to him it symbolized something more. He'd once said my sketch gave him hope. I guess it reminded him of when things were good.

I stepped into his dark room and picked up Will's hope. I kissed the top of his head and gently placed his *twee house* next to his sleeping form. I made my way back down to the living room, feeling solemn and too fucking worn for seventeen. Tears welled in my eyes, but I refused to let them fall. *Hell with that shit.* The paper bag that had held the Chinese food was still on the floor. Frustrated, I kicked it out of my way. A fortune cookie shot out and landed at my feet. I picked the projectile up, ripped the plastic covering off, and slid a tiny piece of paper from the confines of the cookie.

The fortune stayed in my hand, the cookie ended up in my mouth.

Truthfully, I was still hungry. Crunching away and savoring sugary goodness, I read the words on the little slip of paper I held between my fingers.

As I stand before you, judge me not.

It sounded a little hokey and I almost threw the fortune away. But there was something about those words that made me hesitate, something almost prescient. I ended up folding the little piece of paper in half and tucking it in to my pocket. Maybe I needed some symbol of hope just like my brother. I knew the things happening in my life would eventually define my future, and I guess I hoped no matter what occurred those things wouldn't ultimately define me.

My mom came back later that night, but my dad never did.

Jack Gartner had gotten on route 160, heading west to California. But he never made it out of Nevada. His car was found at the bottom of a ravine, below what the officers who came to our door to break the news termed *a treacherous curve*.

Killed on impact, we were told.

Did he lose control, or drive off the road on purpose? Maybe his plan all along had been to leave us and start a new life in California. That's what my mom believed at the time. Still does, in fact.

I, however, am not so sure. My father didn't pack a thing. Sixty dollars and a cancelled credit card, that's all he had on him. I think my dad just gave up. He quit on us, and that was the way he chose to end it. My mom can delude herself all she wants, but I know in my heart that I'm the one who's got it right.

Anyway, the bank took the house soon after my father's death. My mom sold off what little was left. For a while, we became nomads in the desert. We lived in the only big-ticket item that hadn't been repossessed, a white minivan. The Honda Odyssey was home... until Mom won enough money gambling to move us into a cheap apartment. Our new residence was a dump, but at least it had running water. And it was furnished. Kind of.

When we first stepped across the threshold and Mom caught me scowling at the rusty fixtures, the water-stained ceiling, the musty olive-green carpeting, she tried hard to convince me our new place had its good points.

"Like what?" I asked.

"It's close to The Strip. That'll be convenient."

"Convenient for who?" I sniped. "You?"

"Chase," she said pointedly, "it's better than living in a minivan."

She had a point there, so we moved in the next day. Will's first reaction was to run straight to one of the two back bedrooms and hang up his tattered *twee house* sketch. I followed him and watched as he stood on a soiled mattress on the floor—in a shoebox of a room we were going to have to share—and pinned hope on a wall.

After we were settled, time, as it does, marched on. Will and I attended school, while my mom—still fevered and sick with the gambling virus—spent her days in the casinos.

I turned eighteen that April. But no one really noticed. Well, Will did. Not much got by that kid.

He stuck a candle he found in the back of a drawer in the kitchen on a stale snack cake. He made me sit on the only kitchen chair that didn't rock when you shifted, and then he placed the snack cake on a card table we used as a kitchen table.

Will sang me the most beautiful off-key and from-the-heart rendition of "Happy Birthday" that I have ever heard, before or since. When he was done, I leaned forward to blow out the candle. Will stopped me and told me to make a wish first, so I did. And then I blew out the candle. Will clapped and cheered. He asked me what I wished for and I told him it was a secret. I didn't want to tell him I wished for him to be given a better life than what we were, at the time, living. My brother and I split the snack cake in two, dinner for the night, and ate in contemplative silence.

Summer arrived that year and I somehow managed to graduate. But—with my trust fund long gone—college was no longer on the table. With no real guidance, and a lot of pent-up frustration, my downward slide took hold. I was angry all the time, and ended up getting into too many fights to count. The places in Vegas where I'd started hanging were tough. Early on, I got my ass kicked…often.

But then something happened.

I learned how to use my strength, my quickness, *and* my anger. I started to win. I had a real knack for fighting and rapidly turned into a badass nobody messed with. I earned street cred. All that really meant was guys started showing me respect and girls suddenly wanted to have sex with me. I happily obliged more than a few of the latter.

But all that shit meant nothing, I was empty inside. I had no one to talk to about the mixed-up emotions I didn't know how to deal with. Like, why was I so angry all the time? Why did I like to fight so much? Why did it feel so good to make someone else hurt?

But mostly I wondered why I missed my dad so much.

I missed talking to my father, seeing his face every day. I had relied on him, I still needed him. But he was gone. He took his own life. Why couldn't I just accept what had happened and forget him?

But I couldn't, and, worse yet, I longed for answers.

Every day, for a while, in my quest for enlightenment, I'd grab the bus outside our apartment and visit my father. Well, I'd visit his grave. At the head of where my father rested eternally, I'd sit under a big stone angel kneeling by his grave—thankful for the little bit of shade she offered under the hot, beating sun of the desert.

Sweaty and lost, I'd ask her if she could tell me why my dad wasn't still alive. Why had God allowed Dad to take himself away? Why did my father choose to leave me? Why would he leave Mom and Will too? Was our love not enough for him? Did he regret his decision when he realized there was no going back?

Of course, the stone angel had no answers, and one day I just quit going. No more sitting in the shadow of the angel, no more hot and beating sun. No more asking questions that could never be answered.

My trips to the cemetery were over, but that didn't mean I wanted to forget that *someone*—even though he'd left—had once believed in me. Despite everything, I still loved my father and part of me yearned to be just like him.

So, July of that year, I had his angel's likeness—the stone one at his grave—inked in profile on the middle of my upper back, between my shoulder blades.

I shift in the passenger seat now.

I can almost feel her back there, watching over me, like my dad's angel watches over him. And like his angel, mine is kneeling. The edges of her heavy robe lie in a puddle of fabric around her. Her wings are folded against her back. Her hair is long, obscuring the side of her face. And her head is bowed. In supplication or in shame, I haven't decided which. But if she's been watching the shit I've been doing these past two years, it's probably in shame.

After the angel tat healed, Mom hit for more money. I successfully talked her into paying for another tattoo, guilted her into it really. In any case, I ended up with big, intricately detailed wings inked up and over my shoulder blades. The top feathers curve onto my shoulders, while the wings dip down the sides of my back, effectively framing the angel.

But the angel and the wings weren't enough. I wanted something more to remember my father, something to remind me always of that final night, when it was just him and me, eating Chinese food on the floor of an empty home, a last supper shared.

I kept coming back to the cookie, the fortune inside, the hope it symbolized.

As I stand before you, judge me not.

Words printed on a piece of paper, but really they were so much more. So I had those words inked—in concise and script letters—around my left bicep.

My tats were but temporal attempts to heal my soul, as my heart remained an open wound. There was no solace to be had at home. In fact, things were getting worse. I started to drink and do drugs to ease the pain and fill the void. I hated what had happened to our family. Seeing Will transformed from an energetic little boy to a sullen nine-year-old left me sad and frustrated. And watching my mother try to heal her fractured heart with gambling—and eventually men—just pissed me the fuck off.

But at least Mom wasn't indulging in one-night stands like I'd been doing. Nope, Abby actually went out on dates. Still, her attempt at dating led to a revolving door of boyfriends. Some lasted a week or two, some a little longer, but the one common denominator they all shared was that not a single one liked me.

Mom told me to try harder, give these guys a chance for her sake. I laughed and told Abby her men could blow me. "Chase, don't be crude," was her response.

By the end of the summer Mom hooked up with what turned out to be steady boyfriend number three. I was no fool; I immediately sensed my days were numbered. I would've had to have been blind not to see the writing on the wall, a wall I didn't realize I was hurtling toward. But it wasn't just Abby's lame new boyfriend disliking me that was a problem. There was something else, something she'd never admit to. There was no escaping it though, not really.

I saw Abby's problem every day when I looked in the mirror.

Standing in a cramped and steam-filled bathroom, hot water running, can of shave cream poised in hand, I couldn't deny the truth in front of me. I'd swipe at the misted mirror with my free hand, leaving it streaky, but mostly clear. And it wasn't me I saw in the reflection, it was my father. That's how much I looked like Jack Gartner, even at eighteen. And *that* was my mother's real problem.

Shit. Even thinking about it now—two years later—fucks with my head.

I glance over at Tate. He's quiet, taking long pulls from the bottle. I shift in my seat and wind up the window the rest of the way. Time to assess my bleary reflection, time to compare it to what it was, time to compare it to the man who made me…I sometimes do this just to fuck with myself.

When I take in my reflection, I laugh. Hell, the resemblance is still uncanny. And just like when I used to stare at the steamed-up mirror in the bathroom, it's my dad's eyes staring back at me now. But these pale blues are all mine. Yeah, *his* whites were never shot with red like mine.

Still, even with the bloodshot eyes, similarities far outweigh differences. Though it's not *short and tidy*—like Grandma Gartner would like it to be—my hair is the exact same shade as her son's once was, light brown. Jack also blessed me with his straight nose, his square jaw, and his defined cheekbones. Everyone used to say my dad was good-looking, I guess I am too. Girls seem to think so, that's for sure. And my mother sure was smitten with my dad.

Abby used to lean across the front seat of the sporty car my dad bought for himself during the good times. Will and I would be in the back, rolling our eyes at each other. My mom would kiss my dad, making him swerve a little as he drove. She'd tell him he was gorgeous, and that she loved him. Dad would laugh and tell Abby he loved her even more. He'd say his love for her burned hotter than the Vegas sun above us. My mom loved that shit. Will and I, however, would groan in disgust and make gagging noises.

Shit, I feel like gagging now. Not because of the memory, but at how closely I still resemble my dead father. I turn away from my reflection. I can't bear to endure this self-inflicted torture any longer. No wonder I was fucking sent away. Too bad I couldn't disappear completely just as easily right now. Guess, in a way, that's why I live my life the way I do, filling it with drugs…sex…violence.

Back then my very presence in my mom's life must have been a constant reminder of all she had lost. When you're striving to move on, you don't need an anchor to the past. She could move forward with Will, he was just a kid. Besides, he looked like her, not like my father. But I was eighteen, an adult, and far too much my father's son for everyone's comfort. I guess it was just too difficult for Mom to look at me—see *him*—and be reminded of all she'd once had.

So the day steady boyfriend number three, a guy named Gary, told her she could move in with him, I kind of fucking knew the invitation wouldn't be extended to me.

Sure enough, on a blistering hot afternoon, my mom sent Will out to ride his bike and told me we had to talk. She sat me down on the ratty couch in our shitty apartment. I felt like a condemned man waiting to hear his fate, and all the while the noisy air conditioning unit in the window behind me kept blowing gusts of lukewarm air across the back of my neck.

Not that it mattered. I barely noticed. I was mostly numb. In preparation for this "talk," I'd done a couple of lines of coke in my room. Of course, I hadn't brought that shit out until after Will had left. One thing I stuck to was that I never let my little brother see me taking part in any of my newfound vices.

Anyway, that day in the living room, I couldn't sit still. Fidgeting, fidgeting, tapping my foot. Mom took no notice, she was almost as bad. Pacing back and forth in front of me, smoking a cigarette, a new habit she'd just acquired. Gary smoked, so she'd picked up the habit too. *Pathetic*, I remember thinking.

My mother appeared so edgy and wired I almost asked her if she was dabbling in drugs, like me, or if what she had to say was really just that fucking bad. She started speaking before I ever got the chance.

"You're not a kid anymore, Chase," she began, still pacing, ashes peppering the olive-green carpeting.

She took a drag, crinkled her brow, and leaned over to stub her cigarette out in a plastic ashtray on a low table.

"You have to get started on doing something, somewhere, kid," she said as she spun to face me.

She stood right in front of me, and though my head was down I watched her every move. She blew out a breath and I watched her dark blonde bangs lift up off her forehead. A few strands stuck to her skin. Mom was starting to sweat.

"So, Grandma Gartner called the other day," she continued, her words deliberate, pointed, like a knife. "She said she's got lots of room in that old farmhouse back in Ohio. And she sure could use some company."

I looked up at her in disbelief. This woman who'd given me life tried to smile, but she could not. She knew damn well she was spewing pure bullshit. She just wanted rid of me.

"Just spit it out," I ground through clenched teeth, my voice far from even.

"Okay, of course, honey." She looked everywhere but at me. "Uh, so, Gram thinks moving back to Harmony Creek might do you some good, get you out of Vegas, give you a chance to start over, and—"

"Mom, I'm only eighteen. Start over?" I blew out a quick breath. "I haven't even had a chance to get started *here*."

Her expression grew stern. "Chase, don't act like I don't know the things you do behind my back." I tried to protest, but she shushed me. "I know you use drugs. I know you bring girls back when Will's not around. That shit isn't going to fly once we move in with Gary. He won't stand for it, Chase. He has standards—"

I snorted, "The fuck he does—"

"I'm not going to argue with you about it," she said, her voice tired and cracking.

When she reached for her pack of cigarettes, I noticed her hands were shaking. "Honey, I just think Grandma Gartner's is the best place for you right now, okay?"

I picked at a hole in my jeans. "Do I have a choice?" I asked, defeated, and, truthfully, feeling like I'd just been set adrift.

She shook her head no.

I'd known it was coming, but her words still flayed me up the middle and pierced my already damaged heart. I was shocked that my heart could continue beating, since it felt all smashed to hell. But beat it did. In fact, my heart pumped faster and faster, like it was going to burst right out of my fucking chest. Whether my reaction was from cocaine…or despair…I couldn't quite figure.

With my heart pounding like a sped-up death knell, I tried to push some words out of my cotton-dry mouth. "Mom…" I croaked, my voice catching.

I just couldn't finish.

Verbal communication failed me, so I tried to meet her eyes, speak to her soul. Was this really what she wanted? Send her eldest son away? Give up on me? Just like Dad did with all of us.

I searched and searched, but my mother had no answers in her big green eyes, no more than the stone angel had at my father's grave.

Abby took in a stuttered breath and turned away. She swiped at a tear. "It's for the best, Chase," she mumbled.

And then she left me sitting there, all alone, warm air blowing across the back of my neck.

I went back to my room and cut up three more lines.

That was nearly two years ago and here I am. Mom is still in Las Vegas with Will, on steady boyfriend number six, last I heard. She's still chasing the elusive jackpot too, hoping to recapture the life she once knew.

Good luck with that, I think bitterly. *Jackpot, my ass.* If anyone needs to hit a fucking jackpot, it's me.

Suddenly, drug-induced visions of flashing pots of gold swim lazily into my head, along with some break-dancing leprechauns, and I can't help but chuckle.

Tate looks over. He must think my mood has improved, 'cause he starts talking all excitedly about how much money we're going to make from our new business venture with Kyle. I listen to his voice, not really hearing any words, but then the cell buzzes and I am alert, very alert.

Tate tosses it my way. "That there would be the ladies," he says—all smooth like—as I catch the cell with one hand. Even impaired, my coordination is impeccable.

"Ladies, my ass." I roll my eyes.

Tate laughs, knowing as well as I do that the two girls we're meeting up with tonight are no ladies. They're looking for the same thing we are, but therein lies the beauty.

"What's it say?" he asks, nodding to the cell.

The text is kind of blurry, but, then again, everything is. I blink a few times and my vision clears. When I read it out loud, I mimic a high-pitched girl's voice, just to be an ass. "Crystal and I are almost at the lake. Come prepared. Tammy. Laugh out loud, winking smiley face."

"Dude-e-e." Tate shoots me a knowing sidelong glance. "You know what *come prepared* means, right? You got that covered, yeah?"

As reckless as I am—and that's pretty fucking reckless—I always make sure I wrap my shit up. Better safe than sorry. But as I feel around in the pockets of my jeans I realize I've left the condoms at home. "Fuck," I mutter.

The blue *Welcome to Pennsylvania* sign looms ahead, our headlights flashing off the reflective letters.

Tate asks, "What?"

I rake my fingers through my hair. "I forgot the goddamn things at home."

"Not a problem. We'll just stop at the convenience store across the state line."

"Bad idea," I counter. "Cops are always hanging out in there. You think they won't notice how fucked up we are?"

"How fucked up *you* are," Tate corrects, laughing. "I didn't smoke nearly as much as you."

"You smoked plenty," I mumble under my breath.

But Tate is right, I smoked more. And Tate smoked only weed. Plus, my friend didn't see the pills Kyle slipped me before we left.

Still, I nod to the almost-empty bottle. "You pretty much drank that whole thing, dickhead. You'll never pass a field sobriety test."

"Yeah, but I don't plan on taking one, my friend. And, I hide it better than you." He shrugs. "Trust me, I got it covered. Just wait in the car. It'll only take a sec."

Tate's always confident like this. He can talk anyone into just about anything. I always tell him he's a natural-born salesman. Maybe if we ever get our shit together he can do something legit using his smooth ways. It's cool, it's Tate's thing, and it helps make him popular. He's an okay-looking guy—brown hair, brown eyes, kind of skinny—but it's his smooth talk that gets him in with the girls. They eat that shit up.

We cross the state line, turn into the convenience store. No cop cars. "See, we're good," Tate says, still as confident as ever.

I flip up my black hoodie hood and slouch down in my seat. "Just be quick," I mumble.

Tate hesitates, and I know something is up. "What the fuck are you waiting for?" I ask.

He begins his sentence with "Don't be pissed—" and I cut him off right away, hoping I won't have to kick my good friend's skinny ass. It would be a damn shame really, since Tate wouldn't stand a chance against the likes of me. I am way bigger and far stronger, and the rage within me has no match.

"What?" I spit out, clenching my jaw.

Tate ignores my attitude; he's used to it. "I kind of need you to hold on to something while I go in there. Just in case."

"Just in case of what?"

I am running out of patience. I scrub my hand down my face, wary to hear what Tate the salesman is up to now.

He smirks, and I tell him to knock that shit off, save it for the "ladies."

"Okay, okay." He raises his hands in mock surrender. "I may have kind of asked Kyle to give us a little something to get our entrepreneurial gig started."

"Us?" I say, feeling the anger rise up. "You didn't even know I was going to sell with you until about ten minutes ago."

"What can I say, man." Tate places his hand over his heart. "I had faith."

"Whatever."

I try to stay pissed, because what he did was really out of line, but my anger fades fast. High as I am, these strong emotions are too fucking slippery to hold on to for very long.

Tate hands me a plastic packet filled with little pills, a rainbow of color. "Jesus." I know all too well exactly what this shit is. "X? You're fucking higher than I thought. We're supposed to start small, bitch. Move a little bud, see how it goes."

Tate shrugs. "We'll make more money this way. Like, I know we can sell to the girls tonight. Hell, I bet we can talk them into buying *our* hits."

He's laughing at his own ingenuity, but I ignore him. I'm too busy trying to count the pills in the packet. But being in the condition I am in, it's a bit of a challenge.

"How much is this anyway?" I ask, giving up on figuring it out for myself.

"Twenty hits," he tells me, and then he has the balls to throw another packet in my lap. "Make that forty…maybe a little more."

"You're fucking crazy. If we get caught, Tate, this isn't possession. This is possession with intent to sell."

"That's why I'm leaving the shit here with you."

"Oh, that's real fucking cool." Back to being pissed, even my high can't calm me now. I whip one of the packets back at Tate. "I am so not getting caught with forty hits of Ecstasy, asshole."

"Calm down, man." He gingerly picks up the packet I've just thrown and holds it out for me to take back. "If a cop shows up just hit the road."

"What about you?" I ask as I grudgingly accept the X.

Tate grins. "Don't worry about me. You know I can play it cool. Just swing by after the heat's gone, and we'll be back in business."

"The heat? What is this, the seventies?" I ask, laughing, but Tate's already out the door.

I tuck the two packets of Ecstasy into the back pocket of my jeans and think nothing more of it. Until a few short minutes later when a state cop pulls into the lot. Then, I panic.

I start climbing over the console to get the fuck out of there, but, suddenly, with every fiber of my being, I know I've just made the dumbest mistake of my life. That, however, doesn't stop me from slipping down into the driver's seat, throwing the car into reverse. I hit the gas, peel out of the parking lot, and leave a cloud of gravel and dust in my wake.

I've got the Focus up to eighty, music playing…loud, loud, fucking blaring. Maybe I can outrun this cocksucker? I'm tapping my hands on the steering wheel along with the beat, flying so fast it's amazing I don't lose control and crash.

But I don't, I stay steady.

I even make it a good five miles down the road before a cop heading my way—backup, I'm sure—screeches to a wide arced stop in front of me. His patrol car blocks the entire road, so I have no choice but to hit the brakes and squeal to a halt.

My car ends up parallel to the cop car, both of us straddling the lanes, engines idling like we're in some fucking action movie. The air reeks of burning rubber, and smoke billows around us. The speakers beat out a song from 50 Cent that is frankly ironic at this point.

When all the smoke clears, the sign for the lake is right smack dab in front of me. I can't help but laugh. The shit situation I'm in, and all I can think of is that Crystal and Tammy are out there, waiting, for two boys who are never going to show.

Two more cops—including the one from the store—pull up behind me. I pitch the door open, tumble from the seat. I hit the warm pavement and try to stand. Someone yells, "Hold it right there, hands on your head."

I hear guns being drawn, cocked. This isn't a movie, I know they're loaded. I squint to try to see what's happening, but all the flashing lights leave me blinded. Before I can think another drug-muddled thought, someone tackles me from behind. My face smacks right into the yellow center line, but I don't feel a fucking thing.

Whoever tackles me yanks down my hood, frisks me, and comes up with my wallet. Oh, and the forty hits of X, of course.

It's all ambient noise from that point on, but I do hear, "Chase Gartner, you're under arrest."

I have no idea that, despite the altered state I'm in, these will be the last coherent words I will remember for a very long time.

*****

The time following has no sense of structure. Days, weeks, they all blend together. I'm in jail, facing a long, long list of charges. But it's the X that has me fucked.

Bond is set high. I call my mom, but all she does is cry. Like, these horrible wailing sobs that do nothing but make my head ache more than ever. She keeps apologizing for not having the money and swears she'll help me when she can. I hang up. I won't be holding my breath. The past has taught me not to put too much stock into Abby's flimsy promises. Mirages in the desert are what they are—get too close and they disappear.

My grandmother wants to mortgage the farmhouse, all the property around it. We're talking a good fifty-five acres. It'd be enough to make bail, but I tell her *no way*. She's done enough for me already, and look at how I've repaid her. I don't deserve her money… or her love.

So I'm on my own. And not thinking very clearly. Once all the illegal shit is out of my system, I find myself in a constant state of agitation. I can't sleep, I barely eat. I sweat bullets even when it feels like I'm freezing.

Eventually all that passes, but then all I want to do is fight. Like beat heads in. It's worse than when I was back in Vegas; I feel so much more fucking rage. I sit around clenching my fists, hoping for a chance to kick some poor unsuspecting soul's ass.

Finally, my wish is granted.

They throw a cellmate in with me and my ass is on him like an animal, beating the hell out of this never-saw-me-coming sap. But then two guards see what I'm doing, pull me off the bloodied and broken man, and promptly return the favor.

Another blur of pain.

This one, though, I welcome. The medical staff gives me plenty of drugs, legal ones this time. And still more before I am put before the judge.

Even in the sedated fog I float around in, I quickly learn the law... and some new math.

MDMA, Ecstasy—X, as I like to call it—is a schedule I narcotic, and carries as stiff a penalty as heroin if you're caught dealing, which they naturally assume I was. Casual users don't tote around forty-plus hits of Ecstasy, but dealers do.

I say nothing one way or the other to dispel their myth, I rat no one out. I just stay quiet and accept my fate.

My math lesson continues...

Ten pills are equal to one gram, and I've been caught with over forty pills. Forty pills equal four grams, which is more than enough to be charged with possession with intent to sell. But I already knew that part, right?

My lesson isn't over though. It's only just beginning.

I learn in Pennsylvania, the state in which I've been apprehended, four grams can easily earn you a prison sentence. This is especially true when you don't have enough money to hire a good attorney. Add to that, your public defender isn't getting paid enough to care. Not that you're doing much to help the overworked, underpaid man do his job. And, oh yeah, don't forget that one prior arrest for fighting last fall. It didn't seem like much at the time, but it sure haunts your ass now.

Are you keeping up?

Some final math...

Four grams buys you a six-year sentence at a state correctional institute when you have no resources, and, really, no heart to fight it.

Twenty years of age feels like ninety when your freedom is stripped away.

It takes one hundred and forty-three steps to walk down a long, noisy corridor to reach cell block seventy-two.

And when they turn the key, you hear one life—the only one you've ever known up until now—ending.

"It's all about the numbers, man," as Tate would say.

It sure is, my friend. It sure is.

Continue the story...

Available on Amazon: amzn.to/1Ay7ACI